ZEN AND THE ART OF WHITTLING

John Callahan

PublishAmerica
Baltimore

© 2007 by John Callahan.
All rights reserved. No part of this book may be reproduced, stored in a retrieval system or transmitted in any form or by any means without the prior written permission of the publishers, except by a reviewer who may quote brief passages in a review to be printed in a newspaper, magazine or journal.

First printing

At the specific preference of the author, PublishAmerica allowed this work to remain exactly as the author intended, verbatim, without editorial input.

ISBN: 1-4241-4040-4
PUBLISHED BY PUBLISHAMERICA, LLLP
www.publishamerica.com
Baltimore

Printed in the United States of America

Dedication

To my wife Shanah and to my children Samantha, Stephanie, Alexander, and Aaron, I love you all so very much.

Maxims

1) Thirty may not be the beginning of being old but it is definitely the end of being young.

2) Anyone that says, "Hard work never hurt anybody," never did any.

3) If you spend your days carefully watching your step you will never stumble but you will miss life as it passes you by.

4) You don't stop an egg sucking dog by killing all of the chickens.

5) The bigger they are the harder they hit.

6) There is right, there is wrong, and then there is family.

7) If you are doing something for a "thank you," then you are doing it for the wrong reason so don't even bother.

8) Knowledge is power and teachers give it away.

9) If a tree falls in the woods and crushes a philosopher to death, will anyone care?

10) There is no shame in being poor it is just awful unhandy.

11) I work to live I do not live to work.

12) Efficacy is verbosity; efficient is sufficient.

13) You can put out a fire by throwing gasoline on it, but I wouldn't suggest it.

14) I do not understand how anyone that farts can take himself seriously.

15) If you are going to marry a trophy wife you need to have the common courtesy to die before she outlives her trophy years.

16) You know better, so do better.

17) I disregard any directions that contain the phrase, "You can't miss it."

18) Nothing is more foolhardy than attempting to explain to a fool his foolish ways.

19) Sometimes, the squeaky wheel gets replaced.

20) Strive for grace and eloquence not verbosity and pomposity.

Uncle Jess

Uncle Jess was the oldest man I had ever seen. The oldest of my grandmother's eight siblings, Uncle Jess was ancient. At least he seemed that way to a young child that had not seen many elderly people in his short time.

Part of uncle Jess's mystique for me was that he looked exactly the same every time we visited him. His bald head and wrinkled chin were always shaved but both invariably had a good weeks worth of stubble upon them every time I saw him. He had squinted eyes, long ears and loads of loose skin that sagged from his neck.

Uncle Jess was tall and thin, almost as tall as my dad who is six feet two and was always my yardstick for measuring grown-ups. I knew that Uncle Jess was tall, which means that I must have seen him standing on occasions but standing was not his normal pose. He sat either on his porch swing or at his kitchen table, the davenport and easy chairs of the living room did nothing more than hold down the area rug during my visits.

Being Uncle Jess was a lot more than just being old, he also always wore a pair of bibbed overalls. For all I knew, they were the same pair year after year but since his bibs always had a crisp new look about them and since Uncle Jess did not smell particularly bad, that probably was not the case. Attached to a button on his ever-present bibs was a silver chain that disappeared into a tiny watch pocket. Although I had never seen Uncle Jess's watch, my dad also carried a pocket-watch so I imagined an identical watch to be secured to the unseen end of that chain.

Along with his ever-present bibs, Uncle Jess always had a dip of snuff in his mouth. Even at a young age, I was pretty familiar with many different types of smokeless tobacco, but Uncle Jess used something so different and strange from what I had seen other adults use that it was yet another item that set him apart and made him special. Uncle Jess dipped dry, powdered snuff that he stored in a tiny metal canister in the chest pocket of his bibs. He scooped the tobacco from the can and into his mouth with an old, silver baby spoon. The first time I witnessed this ritual it completely blew me away.

The snuff Uncle Jess used was important to me for two reasons. First, I had a deep respect for any man that could take something that looked and smelled so gross and stick it in his mouth. The gross factor was always impressive to me as a lad. Smokeless tobacco is neither for the faint of heart nor weak of stomach. Second, and most important, I was a typical boy and as such I was mystified by the fact that Uncle Jess could spit really far. While sitting with his legs casually crossed on his front porch swing, Uncle Jess could spit, with no visible effort, and clear not only his ten feet of porch, but also the additional six feet of flowerbed directly in front of the porch. If you have never tried spitting for distance, it is hard. Uncle Jess's talent sparked my imagination and encouraged me to more than one wet tee-shirt front as I practiced this skill. I never tired of watching Uncle Jess spit. I was mesmerized by his expectorating prowess and I dreamed one day to achieve perfection like that.

The final characteristic that, above all others, defined Uncle Jess for me was whittling. On that porch swing, in those overalls, spitting those mind blowing distances, Uncle Jess always had a pocket knife in his right hand and a piece of cedar in the left.

Everyone may think that they know what whittling is and how it is done. I have seen it done wrong in enough movies by enough actors trying to portray men from the south, men like Uncle Jess, that I realize just how misunderstood whittling is. In every movie that I have ever seen an actor using whittling as a piece of stage business, the actor was using his knife to cut large chunks out of a piece of wood. Each chunk was cut out of the wood with a strained jerking motion that gave the impression that the actor was trying to make his piece of wood as small as he could as fast as he could. This is not whittling. Whittling is art and as with all art the finished product is not the art. The process is the art.

Whittling is a relaxing endeavor. The act itself is the purpose of whittling not the end product. A whittler will take slow, smooth even strokes with his knife. The resulting product from an experienced whittle stroke will be uniform, paper-thin curls of shavings from your wood. The better the stroke, the tighter the resultant curl. Once again, just as the picture is not the point of painting the curls are not the point of whittling but they are the end result when the whittler is experienced. Just like an art lover can be emotionally impacted by an impressive picture, I have always been struck by the beauty and the uniformity of well whittled shavings.

Uncle Jess whittled so much and he was so good at it that he had five gallon buckets all over his house filled with wonderful smelling cedar shavings. These shavings were so curly and so uniform in size that the buckets looked to be filled with wooden replicas of the springs inside of ballpoint clicker pens.

Now, to be totally honest Uncle Jess's talent at whittling did not impress me nearly as much as his spitting did. Actually, I could not see why someone would spend so much time and effort at a pursuit that was so pointless and boring. After all I had tried whittling, and although I was not allowed to use a knife that was sharp enough to make curls as small as Uncle Jess's curls, I got enough of a taste of whittling to know that it was not for me.

Of course not all answers are apparent to children. Children are explorers out of necessity. They must actively seek out experiences and knowledge because everything is new to them. Children are designed with the drive to be doing some kind of activity to stimulate their minds, which will build the foundation for all future learning and understanding. I could not see the appeal of whittling back when I saw what a large portion of time Uncle Jess devoted to the pastime because I was at a period of my life when most thought was based on collecting information rather than processing it.

As we grow older we retain a good bit of the drive to explore but we also develop the capacity for meditation, introspection, and reflection. So it was in college when I revisited those memories from my youth of Uncle Jess sitting on his porch swing whittling. Amid the pressure of studies and the impending toll that I could feel that student loans would take on my livelihood, I began to see the appeal of such an undertaking. So I left my dorm room and I headed to an area of campus that I had previously noticed cedar trees growing. Breaking a dead branch from one of the trees, I sat on a bench, opened my pocket knife (Everyone in my family carries a pocket knife) and I started whittling. I cleared all of the thoughts in my mind and I concentrated on slow, smooth, even strokes.

After only a few minutes I had entered a calm soothed state of mind. Gone was the anxiety over my classes. Gone was the worry about what I would do with my life after college. Gone was the mounting concern over the debt I had accrued during the previous four years. All that remained was the sun on my skin, a light breeze that rustled my hair and small curls that were not all tight and definitely not uniform but which fell to the ground and got caught by the wind in slow smooth even intervals. Maybe everything would be OK maybe it would not, but stressing about the future would do no good for that future.

I used to think of Uncle Jess as an old man with some interesting quirks. That day on the bench I began to wonder if there was not just maybe a little more to him than that. Maybe he had things pretty well figured out. Maybe he spent his time doing something that soothed his nerves and cleared his mind so that he could better think about the wonders of life, the universe, and everything. Maybe Uncle Jess had reached Nirvana through slow, smooth, even strokes and thin, tight, uniform curls.

A particularly fond memory of Uncle Jess comes from a visit when I was about ten years old. We found Uncle Jess on the front porch swing, of course. The memory from that day would be treasured throughout my childhood and I still treasure it to this day.

My younger sister is a pleasant woman, who can make me laugh and can make me think, but as often is the case between siblings our younger years were not nearly so rosy. By eight years old, Aimee remained the baby of the family and consequently the favorite. Everything she did was cute and special and her evil side was absolutely nonexistent in the eyes of my parents. I could not stand her.

As we approached Uncle Jess, Aimee's shoes caught his attention. She was wearing the cutting edge of shoes technology for the time, in the place where ordinary shoes have laces; Aimee's shoes had two leather bands that folded back on themselves with Velcro to hold them in place.

Uncle Jess set aside his cedar and his knife. He leaned forward from his seat on the porch swing and slowly peeled one of the Velcro bands away from the shoe. He gently reattached the band then peeled it a second time. He reattached the band for the final time then shook his head slightly saying, "Pure laziness."

I grinned from ear to ear and look at Uncle Jess with a kinship I never expected to feel toward any adult, especially the oldest man on the planet. Uncle Jess called my little sister lazy and I absolutely reveled in the rare dig that befell my sister from any lips but my own. I could not see at ten years old that Uncle Jess was not making a judgment on my sister but rather our entire generation. His entire life consisted of hard physical labor. Our lives by contrast consist of such ease and comfort that we cannot be bother by such a grueling chore as tying our shoes.

I am glad of this memory of Uncle Jess. That day I had the rare pleasure of hearing my little sister take some ribbing. Today I get to ponder the deeper revelations that arise from revisiting that moment. I do not think that our "laziness" is a bad quality. I am glad that many larger societal problems have already been dealt with and we are secure enough in the safety and stability of our lives that inventors can spend their days dreaming up easier ways to fasten shoes. I am glad that we have time for such fanciful pursuits like writing, watching movies and playing at the park rather than living only to work, to sleep, and eventually to die. I am glad that I have time to create really clever insults at my sister's expense rather than working all day long and only thinking of her when I see Clydesdales, oxen, and other large footed beasts of burden.

While I am not an avid whittler per se, that moment on that campus benchmarks a turning point in my life. It began an introspection for me, which has lead to a better appreciation of life. In other words it began my adult life; a life that keeps the adventurous pleasure seeking of childhood, but adds the reflection, compassion, and sense of responsibility of adulthood. While I have traded my knife strokes for pen strokes and later for keystrokes,

JOHN CALLAHAN

I still feel an incredible kinship with my Uncle Jess, which goes far beyond the bond of family. No, I do not have it all figured out, but I am thinking about it all of the time.

Free Refills

I am a proud American like most others. During my time as a teacher and while helping my daughters with their grade school homework, I find that much of the patriotism that we feel as Americans is taught to us in primary school. We have a great country and I agree with the prevailing opinion in our public school system that our American children should be taught to take pride in the land of opportunity. I feel that we have a lot to be thankful for in this country and we should be proud of America's rich history of overcoming adversity and triumphing over hatred and negativity. I do, however, like to round out my understanding of and appreciation for the greatness of America from numerous perspectives. I consider myself fortunate to have had so many friends and acquaintances from so many other countries so that I can get an outsider's take on America. I try to get opinions on America from all of the people that I know who were not raised here. Without exception, all of the foreigners that I have met prefer some aspects of their native countries over the way things are done here in America, but they also all speak very highly of the United

States. I had a particularly memorable discussion on the topic with an exchange student from Germany. She lamented the patriotism that abounds in our country. "They play your national anthem at every baseball game. Everyone stands and everyone cheers when it is over." She was not decrying this as an inappropriate practice. She continued with evident frustration, "We could never do something like that in Germany or everyone would be like, 'Oh, you're trying to regain the third Reich'." I am saddened that she feels that her own patriotism must remain subdued.

A colleague of mine is from Nigeria and he said, "America is truly the land of opportunity. People do not know how good they have it. They complain constantly about nothing. Do you know how many people all over the world would love to have so much to eat that they would have high cholesterol?" I have had many encounters with legal aliens and what I have gathered in my unscientific study of non-American opinions about the United States can be best illustrated in a story my friend told me from his first week in America about free refills.

My closest friend during my college years was from the Philippines. Elvin told me that Tagalog is his native language but that English is also widely spoken and understood there. He also explained that while English is widely spoken in the Philippines, it is a dialect so different from what is spoken in America that I probably would not recognize it as English if I heard it spoken. This difference in spoken English came as quite a surprise to Elvin when he arrived in the States. He found that if people spoke slowly enough he could understand most of what they were saying and he could read English fairly well but he was by no means fluent in American English, as he had expected to be.

Elvin moved to the United States in his late teens because his stepfather accepted a job here. The oldest of three boys, Elvin had taken his youngest brother to a popular burger chain as one of their first outings in their surrogate homeland. While looking over the menu above the counter, Elvin's eyes happened upon a phrase that he was certain he was misreading. There was no way that a restaurant could offer free refills on drinks. After reading the phrase several more times he was fairly sure that he was, in fact, reading it correctly but he still could not believe that a place would really give a person more soda for free. It must have been some kind of a ploy to convince patrons to buy more drinks.

Elvin sat eating with his brother who spoke no English and who was too young to read even if he could speak it. Elvin began to explain what he read. He said that he did not really believe that they would refill their drinks for free but he wanted to test it. As teenagers do the country over, and apparently the world over, Elvin convinced his little brother to do the task that might turn out to be extremely embarrassing. So Alex, who did not speak the first word of English, approached the counter with an empty cup to see what would happen. Even without the ability to communicate verbally with the register staff, that little boy got exactly what we all get when we walk to the register with an empty cup, a free refill. With the paper cup clasped firmly in both hands and hoisted triumphantly above his head, he ran back to his older brother shouting the Tagalog version of, "It's true! It's true!"

The United States of America is the land of plenty. We have so much of everything that it is difficult to imagine how awful it would be to go without. We have only to buy one, to get one free. We have all you can eat buffets and bottomless cups of coffee. We get free candy mints with most dinning experiences. My favorite restaurant with all of the delights from south of the border gives complementary *sopapias* at the end of a single meal that contains an entire days recommended Caloric intake. This all leads to another common response to what it means to be American. We are really, really fat.

XXL

It has become fashionable for young people to wear clothes several sizes too large for them. I find it humorous that in the quest to express individuality, teens invariably look exactly like every other "individual" who is constantly pulling up his pants. I, however, have no problem with this particular fad. Today's teens will look back on their teenaged years and cringe at the thought of their saggy britches and untied shoelaces, just as my parents cringe at their bell bottoms and butterfly collars, and the people of my generation cringe at the big hair, ripped clothes, and parachute pants.

Fads come and thankfully fads go. For now, skinny kids in giant clothes are funny to look at. I once saw a kid with the waist of his jeans four inches above the bend of his knees trying to go up a flight of stairs. I'll bet that kid extended my life by a good four hours with the all-consuming fit of laughter I got out of that one. Goofy kids in ridiculous clothes are not the problem I have with XXL clothes. I love to laugh. I hope kids continue to do ridiculous things for the rest of my life. The problem that I have is that I am a large individual, too many complimentary sopapias, and I need clothes of the XXL variety. My problem is that large sized clothes cost more than regular sized clothes. A shirt, any shirt, that can be bought off the rack will increase in cost by three to six dollars for sizes XXL and larger.

As if I did not already have enough on my plate (note the dual meaning) being large enough to need huge clothes, now I have clothing manufacturers telling me that it takes so much material to cover my body that they have to charge me an extra three dollars just to turn a profit. In a time of political correctness and ultra-sensitivity by all people to all forms of exclusion both real and often imagined, the only universally acceptable form of scorn and discrimination left in the United States is against fat people. I prefer the word fat to any of the euphemisms but the word obese is also nice because it conjures frightening images in my overactive imagination.

In schools, kids are reprimanded for teasing others on the basis of sex, color, social status, and mental ability but fat kids get picked on with no repreive. AIDS patients are shown compassion for their lot in life, alcoholics are encouraged to seek treatment for their disease, and fat people are told to, "Save some for the rest of us." The mean little kid inside of most of us knows that pulling little girls' pigtails will likely net a sexual harassment suit but witticisms such as, "Here let me call John...Suey! Pig! Pig! Pig!" will net nothing but laughs all around.

I, like all large people, would love the opportunity to blame my morbid obesity on something anything beyond my control. The truth is I am fat because I eat too much and I exercise too little. I live in America the land of plenty. I can afford to eat more food than I need and I can afford to buy the gas it takes to drive to places rather than to walk. Also, food is good. I love fatty foods and salty foods and sugary foods. In all honesty, if I truly wanted to do something about my weight I probably could. My desire for a nicer looking body does not even come close to my desire for a second sandwich or another handful of cookies.

Airlines want to charge fat people double fares for flying because no one can fit in the seat next to us. I say, go for it. Even if by some miracle of physics you manage to wedge someone into the seat next to me I am confident that they do not want any part of sitting next to the deluge of sweat that is my calling card.

I believe that my personal feelings about my size are pretty well representative of fat people in general. Fortunately, in the land of plenty our penchant for overindulgence can be rectified by medical science, for a price. We can find pills to curb our hunger and support groups to help us come to terms with our "disease." We can even undergo a number of surgeries so vile and disturbing that I dare not go into the particulars here. The mere thought of these surgical procedures is so off putting that it makes a third piece of cheesecake nearly unpalatable.

Bad Words

I have heard before that there are no such things as bad words, only bad intentions. I agree with the premise of this statement and yet there are a number of words that I would prefer that my children not use. A champion of free speech in most cases, I feel that there are instances that legitimize limiting that freedom. I also see in my role as an uncle the need to torment my nieces and nephews and to outrage their parents, my sisters and brothers of both blood and marriage. So in my role as an uncle, I used to tease my sister-in-law that I would teach her two-year-old daughter to cuss. I would make my statement, my sister-in-law would make an overly dramatized protestation and everyone would laugh.

This exchange was an often-used ploy for a laugh at any family gathering. I would state that I would teach my niece to cuss her mother would protest and everyone would laugh. It was not the greatest joke in the world but it was pretty good for hanging out with the in-laws. One day, while driving my niece home after she had spent the night at my house, the joke became much better.

The ride began as most of my rides begin, I found a song I liked on the radio and began to sing along. I then started talking to Haleigh, about those sorts of things that little kids like to talk about; cartoons, toys and candy. With no lead into another topic of conversation Haleigh says in a completely serious tone, "Don't teach me any bad words, Uncle John." This was incredibly cute and I could have left it at the little smile it gave me but I am an uncle and as such I have certain responsibilities.

With a tone of mild shock I said, "Haleigh, I would never teach you bad words. I just say that to tease your Mom but I would never really do it." I gave that a few moments sink in then I added, "Besides, I don't even know any bad words. Do you know any that you could teach me?"

Haleigh sat and thought for a moment and then said, "Um...sex."

I replied, "My, that is an interesting word. Is it really a bad word?"

"Yep."

"Wow, do you know any other bad words?"

"Um...dumb-ask."

"What on earth does that word mean?"

Her reply, "I don't know. Sometimes Mommy calls Daddy that when she's mad."

Now that Haleigh is eight, I think Jessica, my wife's sister, has forgiven me for this conversation with her daughter. I do hope she can forgive my sharing it with a few of my closest friends.

Bad Day

As I stood alone one day at the end of a row of urinals, feet awkwardly placed in order to be clear of the water and other fluids pooled against the wall beneath said urinals; the restroom door opened and a spectacled young man, aged maybe twelve years entered and proceeded to the spot next to me. As he took his stance beside me he made an abrupt jerking motion with his head that I took as a sign of general acknowledgement, perhaps learned from his father, that said both, "Hello" and, "Let us both take care of our business without feeling compelled to talk." I probably have read too much into that gesture because I have tried to create some kind of reasonable explanation for the initial act in the unfortunate chain of events that followed.

Whatever the reason for the forward snapping of his head, the result could not have been anticipated. The young man succeeded in flinging his glasses directly into the urinal hanging on the wall in front of him. The boy was interestingly calm for what would have been an exacerbating incident for me at his age. Without a word he simply stepped forward and reached into the bottom of the urinal.

This story would have been plenty bad enough if he had retrieved his glasses and had only to wash off all of the unmentionable contaminants. However, our hero had no such simple remedy in store that day. As he stepped forward to reach his glasses, he found the unsure ground pooled with the afore mentioned cocktail of fluids causing his forward foot to shoot out from under him. As all of his weight had been shifted to this foot, he fell forward headfirst. The top of his head narrowly missed the bottom of the urinal but could not miss and did not miss the cinder-block wall. As the crown of his head struck the wall with a hollow "thunk" his body crumpled into a half fetal position and came to rest in the mess on the floor.

At this moment I had been acquainted with the boy for all of three seconds but I was concerned for his well being nonetheless and I was more than a little amazed by what I had just seen. I selected the must empathetic voice I could muster and asked, "Are you all right?" The words sounded weak and meaningless in my own ears. All was obviously not right with this young man. As a matter of fact there were several things wrong at that very moment. Still, what else could I have done? We always ask, "Are you alright?" when we really mean, "I can plainly see that all is not right but I want to know to what extent things have gone wrong for you today. I want to know, for example, if you feel that medical attention will be necessary or if there is anything that I can do to help you feel less 'Not all right.'" Perhaps he understood that this is what I meant when I ask, "Are you all right?" but it felt inadequate nonetheless.

The boy drew himself up to one elbow and said simply, "Whoa, bad day." He then favored me with a small crooked grin and the set about the task of standing up and retrieving his glasses. I was struck immediately with the incredible outlook on life I witnessed in this child. I know adults numbering too many to count that could not have put the true significance of this ordeal into perspective at all, much less so quickly. I know for a fact that at his age I could not have shrugged off such an incident so quickly and so completely. At best I would have been searing with embarrassment that someone had witnessed the ordeal and to be quite honest I would have probably started crying from that embarrassment. I would be able to laugh off something like that today but at twelve years old it would have been impossible to get out of a situation like that without a few swear words and without dusting off my indignant tough guy persona for the benefit of the old guy that was taking a pee next to my head.

The boy amazed me at that moment and he amazes me still as I think about him now. What is more, he makes me wonder how many things in my life can be swept away with a crooked smile and a, "Whoa, bad day." If he can be wise beyond his years and understand that the incident in the restroom is of little consequence in the grand scheme of things, can I be wise beyond my own years and realize that while the things that cause worry and stress in my own life may be of more consequence than slipping in a public restroom, they are not important enough to dwell upon, to hold me back, or to keep me awake at night. I learned a life lesson from a twelve-year-old boy. It was a lesson that I had already learned, don't sweat the small stuff, but it is a lesson that has new depth for me today because of a soaked young man that fished his glasses out of a urinal and went on with the business of his life.

Cryogenics

Is there anything creepier than the idea of an ice chest filled with frosty corpses? No horror writer's wonderfully inventive tale of terror has ever given me half the willies I get when I think about cryogenics. There are a series of erroneous assumptions made on the way to the great ice nap and I would like to dissuade those currently riding the fence about whether or not suspended animation is the right choice for them.

Error number one is the thought that, "It is my life and my body and I should have the final say about what happens to me when I die." There is a degree of indignity in death, which cannot be helped. No one gets to choose how or when he meets his natural demise. There is the peaceful, and enviably dignified, death in one's sleep at one end of the spectrum and there is dying of dehydration from uncontrollable diarrhea, like Thomas Jefferson, at the other end of the spectrum. The only redemption available to those unfortunate soles like our founding father is to arrange to have the mortal coil disposed of in a respectable manner that will allow one's family to put a bit of closure to the grief over their loss. A

Pappa-cicle is not the way for a child to come to terms with the father's death. What we must understand is that we are dead. The rituals and ceremonies associated with death are not for the dearly departed but rather they are for the survivors of the deceased intended to allow the gathered mourners to share and express their sadness. No one wants to attend a funeral with the phrase, "What the hell was he thinking," running through the mind throughout the entire service. Every accomplishment, every kindness, every good deed will be instantly erased and replaced by awkward musings and backhand whispers. Your final say must consider the needs and emotions of those you leave behind.

Error number two is putting one's trust in the "scientists" who run the great cryogenics scam. What a money making swindle. "We're gonna freeze ya and keep you cool all for the unbelievable bargain basement price of $28,000. Then some day we're gonna thaw you out and fix the problem that killed you." This is about as scientific as cutting off your testicles so you can hitch a ride on the spaceship that is following the Hale-Bopp comet. I can hear the protests of the cryogenics faithful now, "In the future, there will be cures for all kinds of diseases that we have today. In the future, scientists will be able to thaw us out and cures our ailments so that we may live full and healthy lives." I must admit that in the future there probably will be the technology to thaw you back out and to remedy all of your infirmities but there is one huge problem that this argument is not taking into account and that is error number three.

The final error in judgment that precludes cryogenics from consideration for anyone in full command of his faculties is as follows. What would people of the future possibly want with you? Why would the societies of 50, 100, or 500 years down the road possibly want you in their world? The very best case scenario would be that you have a first hand account of history. Who wouldn't love the chance to revive Abraham Lincoln, Fredrick Douglas, or the afore mentioned Thomas Jefferson and talk to him about what he did and what he thinks? My guess is that anyone that got the chance to talk to a favorite historical figure would regret that opportunity. All three of these men are held upon pedestals in our minds and they are revered by history. I think that meeting any of them could be nothing but a disappointment because at the end of the day they are all only men and they cannot possibly live up to our expectations of them. Ideals are incorruptible; people are disappointing.

I may be wrong here thinking that these three men or anyone else out of history would be a disappointment. They may meet and exceed our every expectation. Even if I found aspects of their personalities to be off putting I would still like the opportunity to talk to any of them, along with a long list of others, if I were afforded that option. Even if I am wrong about the disappointment of the heroes of history it does not diminish my point because not one of these men is cryogenically frozen. The frozen folks have names like John Q. More-Money-Than-Sense. How many of the frosty corpses, once reanimated, would have even a cursory knowledge of anything of interest to anyone in the future?

I mentioned our expertise on present day current events as a best-case scenario and I think that all other scenarios go downhill from there. People are not going to ask questions like, "What was war?" The big stuff will be covered by the history books. The questions that the future might hold for my contemporaries would be about impressions of first hand experiences.

"What was the president of your day really like?"

"I don't know I never met him. But I heard he was a cheerleader and doesn't that pretty much say it all?"

"How did hurricane Katrina impact your life?"

"It was awful. I had Joe Horn on my fantasy team and I couldn't unload him for nothing."

"What was it like to live in a country that put so much emphasis on the military and so little on education?"

"Hey! The Asian kids knew that if they didn't let me copy we would kick 'em out of the country and bomb their country back to the stone-age."

"Is there anything else that you would like to add so that we may better understand our culture and heritage of the past?

"I really don't understand what your saying but I gotta say, I really though we would have been able to cure ugly by now. I guess with all the diseases you guys were curing you didn't have time to address the problems that were truly important to us."

This may not be the way it would go but honestly, how many of us have truly desirable first hand knowledge? The future does not want us. The future is better off without us. You may want to live forever but no one else wants you to. Let it go. If you are kooky enough to seriously consider freezing your corpse, your life is probably not fulfilling enough to need to return to it after death.

I Done

Alexander, my two year old, loves the lights in the bathroom of our house. He loves them because the two switches in the bathroom are the only two in the entire house that are low enough for him to reach. In the days and weeks follow the discovery of the bathroom switches he spent all the time he could in the bathroom turning the lights on and off. While his initial excitement over the lights has departed he still takes pleasure in turning on the second light when I enter the bathroom with him and turn on only one.

Another great joy in Alexander's life is bath time. He delights in filling cups and pouring the water out again. He also enjoys a rubber ducky and a boat in his bath time play but the lion's share of his attention is lavished upon the simple cup that is in the bath to rinse his hair. As all parents know children will give simple objects more attention than the most extravagant toy. When Alex is not busy marveling at the water holding properties of a cup, he can usually be fond sitting in his emptied toy box.

The only part of my son's life that is detrimental to me is his inability to sleep through the night. Now granted my wife takes the majority of the nightly wake up calls but I have been known to make an occasional night round. I always glance at the clock on these nights in a haphazard attempt to keep track of how much sleep I am losing. This habit is the reason I know that it was 3:30 AM on the night that Alexander came into my room and said "Daddy." I remember thinking to myself, "At least he isn't crying." Alex is a happy and carefree child most of the time but he rarely wakes up in a good mood.

Fortunately, Alex is a bit ahead of the curve in the speech department so I can ask him what he wants, he can tell me, and then I can get it and go back to bed. Usually he wants milk, which mysteriously he pronounces, "Lilk," even though he can say many other words that start with m as in, "More lilk!"

I sit up and I say, "Hi buddy, what are you doing up?" Alex responds with the worst two words any sleep starved parent can hear, "I done."

Knowing that it would not work and that I would be up for quite some time but trying it anyway I said, "No sir, you're not done. You need to get back in bed and go night, night." To my utter amazement he gives me his long drawn out, "Oookaay." I tuck Alex into bed, I kiss him and I get back into my own bed with the clock reading 3:32 AM two minutes being a personal record for a late night service call for my son. I should have known that I was not going to get off that easily.

An indeterminable amount of time later, I was startled awake by a peculiar sound. I bolt up in bed and said, "What the hell?" mostly so my wife knows that I am selflessly getting up a second time in the same night to take care of business. The sound was not peculiar because I could not place it, the sound was peculiar because there was no way that I should have been hearing it at 4:30 AM. That sound was a splash. As I sat in bed, trying to get a handle on why I would hear a splash at this time of the morning I realize that there is another sound coming from the same direction as the splash. This second sound began to fill the gaps in my sleep-slowed mind as I made the trip across the bedroom to the door. I opened the door and found the hall was ablaze in the light of both fixtures in the bathroom.

As I stepped into the bathroom I beheld an amazing sight. As I had already discerned, the second sound was a sink faucet spraying into a full water basin. Alexander had his two big toes holding him up off of the toilet seat and his chest and torso were lying across the sink. Luckily, a washcloth had fallen into the washbasin plugging the drain and allowing the basin to fill for Alex's enjoyment. Unfortunately, Alexander did not feel the need to turn the water back off once the basin was full. Judging by the amount of water on the bathroom floor the idea to explore the bathroom alone must have occurred to Alex very shortly after I put him in bed and fell back to sleep myself. Like every parent my thoughts revisit this night and tally the ever increasing number of ways that Alex could have gotten hurt but now that the bathroom is dry and the boy has come out unscathed I can look back on that night and smile.

When I knew that everything was OK, I was able to ask with no fear in my voice, "Alexander! What are you doing?" His answer of course, "I done." Alex then went and got into bed with his Mom. She changed a very soggy diaper and they went back to sleep. I joined them at 5:34 AM knowing that it could have been worse.

Bring Out the Chains

Autumn is my favorite season. The blistering hot days of summer are gone and the bitter cold days of winter are still months away. I like the crisp dry air on a cloudless starry night. I like when the grass goes dormant and I no longer have to mow the lawn. I like the crinkle crunch of dry leaves beneath my feet and the wisps of steam that accompany my breath on cool autumn nights. I like bonfires, and corn-mazes, and haunted houses, and a return to school for the kids. I like so many aspects of autumn that I cannot possibly name them all but the most exciting part of autumn is the return of football. I like to watch football, and talk about football, and even play a little football when the opportunity presents itself.

I know what you are thinking, my wife landed quite a catch. Right? Well, I try not to bore her with my football interest and besides she does not seem to mind talking about a little football every now and again, although she could just be placating me.

The start of football season has special significance for me because there are only two sports that I enjoy watching, football and hockey. The end of football season and the beginning of hockey season overlap so there is no sense of loss and longing from one to the next. There is, however, a considerable lag between the end of hockey season and the beginning of football season. I try to fill the void and watch all the guys driving their endorsement-laden machines around in circles but I still have my full complement of teeth and the sport makes no sense to me. I once heard a baseball game described as three minutes of action crammed into two hours and, frankly, I find that to be a generous assessment. So, I am generally pretty excited and ready for some sports entertainment by the time football season rolls around.

Football is the embodiment of the classic struggle of good versus evil. While no team is literally evil, we fans are able to attribute wickedness to the arch rivals of our favorite team just as easily as I am telling you right now that the team from up north is treacherously, diabolically evil. GO BUCKS! We are able to vicariously experience the thrill of victory if our team prevails, and we can blame poor officiating if our team loses.

Officiating football is a thankless and stressful job. For me, there is no moment more stressful in a football game than when a tackle is made very near the first down marker and the officials need to bring out the chains. With purpose in their walk/jog two officials, the keepers of the chain, trot onto the field and into the spotlight.

Tension mounts as the painfully slow process unfolds. The referee kneels and places his hand on the ball. The front keeper of the chain pulls his stick several feet above the ground, stretches the chain taut, and then thrusts his stick ground ward next to the football. At this point one of two scenarios plays out.

Either the football is slightly farther downfield than the stick or the stick is farther down field than the football. This game of yards is reduced to a game of inches and one team is elated while the other is deflated. Personally, I am fine with both scenarios even when the outcome goes against my team. I try to remember that it is just a game and the champion of the contest does not truly matter in the grand scheme of life. I am truly impressed and amazed by one aspect of the chain ritual. At these moments of measurement in the middle of this game that epitomizes manliness; the referee, *senior numero uno* as far as football officials go, is willing to admit that he is unsure of what the correct call is to be made and that he needs someone else's help in making the decision. Needing help and asking for help are not *macho* and I am always impressed when a measurement is asked for.

Where I run into real problems with the taking of the measurement is in an aspect of the procedure that I have never heard another soul question. When a measurement is requested it is obvious that the referee does not know what the measurement will yield. Similarly, the keeper of the chain handling the front stick has no idea where the sticks tip will come to rest after the chain has been pulled tight, he only knows that the pulling of the chain must be done at chest level and then ceremoniously lowered while the fans wait with bated breath. My problem is that there is never any question about where the rear stick man should place his marker. It is possible for a play to end at the opposite end of the field from where the keepers of the chain keep the official first down distance. The width of a football field is fifty yards and yet at the end of his walk/jog the rear keeper of the chain knows *exactly* where to put his stick down. His stick placement is never one inch closer to the end zone or one inch farther from the end zone than it is supposed to be.

The man in charge of officiating the entire game does not know where the stick will fall and whether or not a first down has been achieved. The guy holding the front stick has absolutely no idea where his stick will land until he pulls the chain tight and places his marker. Yet the rear keeper of the chain knows the precise placement for his stick even from distances up to fifty yards away. He never misses his spot even by a single link of the chain, which is often the difference between first down and change of possession. I am not sure how much a rear keeper of the chain makes but he deserves a raise.

So, why not fire the fool holding the front stick? He does not deserve the title keeper of the chain since he has absolutely no idea what is going on in the game anyway. We could remove the chain all together and let the rear keeper of the chain become the sole stick holder. Now when the ball is downed too close for an accurate call to be made from the field the referee can look to the sideline at the sole keeper of the stick who would respond with something along the lines of, "He missed it by two links." Of course there is no longer a chain and technically no links but we would keep this phrase around as a bridge to the past in much the same way that left handed baseball pitchers are still called "South Paws" even though home plate no longer necessarily points west in all stadiums.

The method of allowing the sole keeper of the stick to make his calls from the sideline would speed up the game by removing the time wasting ritual of the walk/jog from the sideline and the flourish from the front keeper of the chain extending his TV face time with his unneeded chain pulling ceremony. I image that part of the reason for keeping the chain measurements as part of the game is that it adds drama and suspense to the football game. We could keep that drama aspect by allowing the sole keeper of the stick to trot onto the field while the referee kneels with his hand placed upon the football. The sole stick holder could prolong the suspense by waving the sole stick teasingly around in front of his chest before placing its tip on the field of play in exactly the spot that it belongs.

Doctors

I was once given a particularly insightful piece of advice while I listened to a rant about how troublesome it is to follow the restrictive lifestyle prescribed by a doctor. At the end of the complaining session I was told, "Of course I'll do whatever he wants me to do. What's the use of going to a doctor if you don't do what he tells you to do?"

This statement struck me as extremely profound. We seek out the advice of a professional but we are reluctant to take that advice if it is difficult or inconvenient. A doctor has the patient's best interest in mind when a plan of action is prescribed. Be it improving ones diet, increasing ones physical activity, or eliminating ones vices; a doctor gives the best plan of action for a long and healthy life. In spirit, this suggests that we should seek out a doctor's advice and follow it to the letter. In practice, I avoid going to see a doctor at all costs. After all, what is the point of seeing a doctor when I know that I am not going to do what he wants me to do?

Even in my youth, I avoided doctor visits. In junior high when I went to my family doctor for a physical to join the track team, my doctor marveled at his records and told me that I had not been in to see him in six years. This is not to suggest that I had not sought medical attention in those six years. I had my share of visits to the emergency room for the occasional stitches and once to have a bone reset; however, I did not have the need for a general practitioner. To be fair, most need for doctors falls to infants and the elderly but I have had times in my adult life when I should have gone to the doctor and did not. On the Fourth of July weekend a few years ago, I had the worst illness of my life. For a period of about twenty-four hours I felt so bad that not only was it a chore sitting up, but I had to lay on my back with my head tilted back and to the left because this was the only position in which I did not feel nauseated to the point of dry heaving. The lowest point of this illness was when I awoke with the need to have a little sitting time in the restroom. The thought of getting out of bed was so intimidating that I seriously considered soiling myself just to save the ordeal of getting up. Eventually, I reasoned that it would take even more time out of bed to clean myself up than it would to drop the proverbial deuce.

This low point would have been a wakeup call to even the most terrified doctor phobic. I, however, reasoned that while I should go to the doctor, I do not feel well enough to manage the car trip to the hospital. Although, I had taken a couple of rides to the hospital with the rescue squad, I had had blood spurting from one appendage or another on those occasions and the thought of calling an ambulance either never crossed my mind or if it did it was dismissed as an excessive measure. I assume that I had the flu that Independence Day weekend. I have never before had the flu but my Dad described it to me once as feeling so bad that you would have to get better in order to die, and that definitely describes how bad I felt that weekend.

My avoidance of doctors is apparent when one knows the lag time between the doctors that I referred to as, "My doctor." The family doctor of my youth died my senior year of high school and I did not get another doctor until eight years later. In all honesty I would probably still be doctor-less if it were not for the insistence and the persistence of my wife. (However, she really dropped the ball in her nagging duties one Independence Day weekend.) I am the type that hopes for an appointment a few days away so that I can cancel the appointment if my symptoms give even the slightest sign of diminishing.

I do not avoid doctors out of fear or pride. It also is not a lack of trust in my doctor or any other doctor for that matter that keeps me away. I know that my doctor will do his best to make me as healthy as I can be. I also find my doctor to be a pleasant man that is very thorough in his work. The reason why I avoid doctors is because they practice medicine. The medical field is not an exact science. There are no sure-fire cures devoid of hidden costs. The unknown side effect possibility is not something that I can let go of. I can never un-remember that doctors used to prescribe Thalidomide for morning sickness. This was not done out of spite but pure old-fashioned ignorance. I do not blame doctors for not knowing but I do not trust medicine and I cannot overcome this mistrust.

All medicines are suspect. One needs look no further than a favorite magazine to know that for a one page advertisement for some new wonder drug there are two pages of disclaimers. We owe our longevity to modern medicine. We have a longer and better quality of life than any other period in human history due in large part to dedicated doctors and medical researchers. I know that I am better off for modern medicine but I also know that the answers to all of life's problems will not be found in easy to swallow gel-caps. I am probably lucky that I did not die that Independence Day weekend and I know that modern medicine was there to try to save me if I had gotten any worse. I am also much better about seeking medical help and advice, per spouse's orders, than I have been in the past. Now I listen to what my doctor has to say and I then ignore the advice if the consequences of dismissing it do not appear to be life threatening. This is of course my answer to the opening question. What is the point of going to see a doctor if you are not going to do what he tells you to do? Why, the point is to be sure that ignoring his advice will not kill me.

Fireworks

I cannot say as I remember enjoying fireworks as a child as much as I enjoy watching my children enjoy them now. I have vague memories of sitting on a red, white, and blue crocheted blanket with Mom, Dad, and my two sisters. I remember the grass poking up through the holes in the crocheted blanket and itching my legs. I remember the boom of the non-lighted charges rattling through my chest signaling that the display would start in five minutes.

One memory I have of my childhood fireworks watching is the finale. I could not believe that something so obviously expensive would be put on display in such a hedonistic rush rather than savored one at a time like the rest of the show. The sky was beautiful during the finale. The crowd cheered during the finale. I learned a lot about giving the people what they want from fireworks. I also learned that some things were better in an overwhelming rush rather than carefully horded and systematically "enjoyed" in a process as long and drawn out as possible. — I feel the need to point out that this is the exact opposite of the change of heart that most children experience. I always tried to prolong any experience that was good. I often drew out many experiences so long that much of the enjoyment was lost as a result. — I experienced the excitement of the crowd and I began to realize that this energy was not something that could be summoned by an individual. True flights of fancy can only be experienced by a mob.

My clearest memory of fireworks is of the mad dash to the cars during the finale. An interesting aspect of the personality of the mob is the uniformity of movement. Some people got up and began their run as soon as the finale began. Most watched the majority of the finale and then with no signal or prelude began running as one body. I assume that some stayed until the very end but I cannot be sure. A fireworks finale is definitely a rare and special and powerful event because I remember seeing my mother run during the finale, which is something that I have never seen in any other context in my life. We all ran Mom, Dad, my sisters, and me. There is something unforgettable about running through a cemetery, which butts up against the park, at night with your family and a crowd of strangers where most of the adults are carrying lawn chairs and blankets while we are constantly backlit by colorful explosions in the sky. I did not know the word juxtaposition at the time but these discordant activities combine to create one of the most vivid memories of my childhood. Incidentally, during this run the crowd is still cheering over the brilliance of the finale.

Skip ahead ten minutes and my family and the rest of the mob are all in our cars in the bumper to bumper traffic trying to leave the display area at precisely the same time. To this day I can remember the excitement of the crowd during the finale, though not the fireworks themselves. I remember the people carrying blankets and lawn chairs through the cemetery and I remember the red brake lights of my first traffic jam.

From yesterday with my children I have completely different memories of the Fourth of July. I started the morning with a reading of the Declaration of Independence. (Yes it must suck to be the child of a Social Studies teacher.) Later, I taught my kids, my nieces, and my nephew how to play croquet at a family picnic. By evening at the park I sat in the deepening dusk and watched my kids play with the glow sticks my wife bought for them. They threw them into the air, they ran, they giggled, and they made me happy to be alive. At least two dozen times I invited my son to join me on the dark side as he pummeled me with his, "Light saver." I remember the ooing and the aahing of my children during the entire display.

I am not sure what, if anything, my kids will remember of the Fourth this year. They will not remember a mad dash to the car, however, because we stayed until the very end. One of my life lessons that I learned very well is that it is better to be leisurely when you can afford to be leisurely and to only hurry when you must. I marveled at the explosions of laughter from my children as they marveled at the explosions of color in the sky and I held this truth to be self evident, this is what Independence Day is all about.

Liar

An odd series of events happened a couple of days ago. One of my fourteen-year-old daughters, Samantha, has been baby-sitting her young cousins during summer vacation. My sister-in-law left twenty-five dollars on a stand in the living room for Sam when she picked up her children after work. Samantha, being my daughter, was too busy watching TV to pick up the money and safely tuck it away.

At 4:00PM the following day, I was home sick, I hear Samantha exclaim, "Where's my money?" It is explained to me then that Samantha owes $2.50 to her twin sister Stephanie, which is the apparent basis for the follow up questions directed at Steph, "Do you have my money?" and "Can I check your purse to make sure?" Stephanie agreed to the search of her purse and I began to assist Samantha searching for the money on the floor under the stand and behind the couch. All the while I am gently reminding Samantha—read lecturing—that she must keep better track of her belongings, as well as possibly apologizing to her sister for the implication that

Stephanie has stolen anything that belongs to Samantha and comes up missing. During our search Alexander, two months from his fifth birthday, comes over to watch the commotion and I ask him, "Do you know where the money is that was on this table?"

Alex's answer was, "Yeah, I picked it up so it wouldn't get lost."

At this point I am a little peeved over the lie about the reason he picked up the money but I do not let it show because at least he immediately owned up to taking the money. Also, we could discuss how stealing is wrong and what we should do in the future. This was going to turn out to be a fine teachable moment and no real harm was going to come of it. This event was going to have to end one common practice in the household, Alexander has been allowed to put money he finds around the house into his piggy bank where it becomes his money. Up until this point he has unfailingly asked if he can put the money he finds into his bank but we will have stop allowing that to happen.

"What did you do with the money?" I asked.

Alex responded, "I put it back on the stand."

I said, "Well, it's not on the stand now, maybe you put it somewhere else. Let's check your pockets since that's a handy place to put money."

We check all of Alexander's pockets and there is no money. Alex says to me, "It was not even in my pocket. Why did you say it was in my pocket, Dad?" I explained that I just wanted to check his pockets but that I do not really know where the money is and that is why I asked him where it was.

I asked again, "Do you know what happened to the money?"

Alex replies, "I took it back into my room to put it in my piggy bank but I couldn't find it so I put it in the bottom of my toy box."

As we head back to his bedroom I began casually asking Alex questions trying use this teachable moment while we retrieved the money. "Alex," I asked, "What is money good for?"

His answer, "To pay for things."

I then asked, "And what things do you want to pay for?"

He holds up two fingers while he says, "I just need two jets."

Changing approach I asked, "Whose money was on the stand?"

"Sammie's," he said.

"Can you just take Sam's money?"

"No," he says, "I should not steal Sammie's money. That is for her to pay for things and she will be sad if I take it."

Alex and I began slowly emptying his toy box while we talked. He had begun to tear up a bit while talking about his sister's disappointment over his taking her money. I had decided on his punishment and so I said to him, "Son, I am glad you told me about taking Sam's money but you know that it was wrong so you are going to have to lose two game days." We have a video game system that Alexander loves a little more than I would like. Rather than overreact to his gaming obsession and throw away the games my wife and I have designated Tuesdays and Saturdays as game days. Thirty minutes for a maximum of twice a day Alex is allowed to play video games.

The expression on Alexander's face reveals that he has just heard the most horrible and perplexing news of his young life. "But why!?" he wailed as his misty eyes instantly welled with huge tears.

I respond, "Son, if you do something wrong you must have consequences." He grudgingly agreed that some punishment was in order.

As we continued to remove toys from the toy box Alexander tells me, "Did you know that there is a bad Alex? He lives in a house just like my house and he has a Mommy and a Daddy and a Sammie and Stephie only he doesn't know better like I do. He lives right here just like I do. I think he took the money."

I said, "Well son, we need to find that money and return it to Samantha." We got to the bottom of the toy box and there was no money.

Alexander looks at the bottom of the empty toy box and says to me with a hint of hopefulness in his voice, "Maybe I didn't take Sammie's money."

I replied, "Alex, why would you tell me you did something when you really didn't?"

He said, "I can't remember everything I do."

Not satisfied with the explanation I got I wanted to check his train box for the money. Alexander has such an obsession with a certain British tank engine that he has a separate smaller toy box for his numerous creepy faced trains and tons of snap together sections of train track.

I slide the train box toward me and I begin removing the pieces of track. Still crying Alex says, "Can we please stop? I did not take the money."

I asked, "Are you tired of looking in your toys?"

"Yes, I'm tired of looking in my toys and I didn't take it." It was just about time for my wife to get home from work and in my sick state I was getting tired so I told him we can put his toys back into his box and ask his mom about the money.

When my wife got home I ask her, "Did you do anything with Sam's money?"

"Yes, I put it up so it wouldn't get lost."

In my youth, I lied to my parents a lot. Never did I lie to get myself into trouble. I asked, "Alex, why would you tell me you did something when you did not do it?"

His response was, "I didn't want you to be mad."

I am not sure what this answer is supposed to mean but I did not press the issue since clearly Alexander can completely fabricate an incredibly detailed story and deliver it in a manner that I cannot discern from the truth. Alex enjoys telling me stories while I type them. His stories normally mix characters from several established books, movies, and television series. His stories are definitely original even though the characters are not but I have never worried that he could not distinguish reality from fantasy.

I think that our adventure into the world of the bad Alex was probably due to an incomplete understanding of the truth. The increased exposure to his cousins during Samantha's sitting has increased the number of lies Alex has told recently. I believe Alex may think telling the truth might mean saying you did something that you should not have done regardless of whether or not you really did it. I may never know for certain why Alexander did this but he was ecstatic that his two game days were reinstated. After hearing this story, one of my friends at work assured me that Alex will be published before I ever am.

EOE

I am a white, Anglo-Saxon, Protestant, male heterosexual. Historically, the preceding attributes were requirements for most good jobs in America. Equal opportunity employment addresses the inequities of the past by ensuring that my application for any job is automatically placed at the bottom of the application pile. I am the absolute last candidate to be considered for any position. It does not matter that I am an excellent employee with a strong work ethic. Also, my qualifications for any position are unimportant. All that matters is that the workforce resembles the rich multicultural, patchwork quilt that is the American populace.

Does preferential treatment today really make up for exclusionary practices of a bygone era? I know that hatred, racism, and bigotry exist today but none of them are the prevailing attitudes that they were historically. Are we incapable of running a meritocracy in this country? Discriminating against one group today does not fix discrimination against other groups in the past.

Running a quota system is degrading. The worst part is that the person who gets a job, any job, is qualified for that job the vast majority of the time. I have only encountered a very small number of people in my working experience that truly had no business in their position. No matter how qualified someone is for a job s/he will be resented by the people passed over for the position. If the job recipient is from a minority race, religion, ethnic group, sex, creed, or some other qualifier the notion is that the employer was just filling a quota. If I get a good job it is good-old-boy cronyism at work and my skills and ability to do the job well do not come into play. I, personally, have struggled to get a good job. I have been passed over and flatly rejected for, conservatively, 400 jobs in the past ten years. I am constantly networking and searching for that next great career move because that is what it takes to get ahead in the real world. No one hands me anything. I research it, I work for it, and I take what I can get. I have never felt that I was owed anything because in reality no one is owed anything.

I have heard people in their twenties speaking seriously about reparations. "We never got our forty acres and a mule." How dare you say we? Someone born in the 1980's has no business laying claim to something that was intended to repay abuses against people that lived 140 years ago. I have seen college graduates refuse to work in a factory because their education makes physical labor beneath them. Many people feel that things should go their way. Why are we lawsuit happy in America? Because it is easier to sue for a living than it is to earn a living. I was burnt by coffee you sold me so you owe me something. My heavy smoking, high cholesterol, model of poor health husband died on your operating table so you owe me a free ride. The true problem in America is not the systematic racism and sexism of our past, it is the feeling of entitlement that permeates our culture of today. People think that the things they want should be easy to get. Life is tough and it should be tough. The things that come easily are not appreciated, which is why entitlement programs have done nothing—domestically and abroad—to improve the long-term quality of life for their recipients.

In my career of working with the underprivileged I have had ample opportunity to see the cycle inherent to entitlement programs. What kinds of children are raised by welfare recipients? Most children continue the cycle of early pregnancies and public assistance. There must be a better way. What kind of life can a child expect when it is born into poverty and born to parents not mature enough to properly meet that child's needs. I know what kind of life such children can expect because I have worked with teens and adults from just this kind of household for most of my adult life. I have worked in juvenile detention homes and prisons for long enough to know that entitlement programs perpetuate poverty and they perpetuate criminal thinking. The people that speak to me most often about reparations are prison inmates. These men have spent their entire lives trying to get something for nothing. Selling drugs, stealing, robbing, and extorting are all ways to get the money you want without working for it. The vast majority of crime is committed out of greed not need. I am entitled to a rich glamorous lifestyle and I need not work for the life I want because it is owed to me. Physical labor is degrading and beneath me. I deserve more.

Our "cure" for the injustices of the past is just as bad and degrading as the problems it was meant to fix. The real fix for this entire mess that our society has created is accountability. If everyone were truly held accountable for their actions and were made to restitute their misdeeds we would begin to solve the problem that the spirit of entitlement has exacerbated. We, the multi-talented, multicultural middle class are tired of carrying the dead weight of the leeches to our system. The system itself has created a class of people incapable of pulling itself out of the mire of public assistance. As a matter of fact, the system penalizes people who attempt to get out of the system by dropping assistance as soon as a person makes any effort to help himself. Entitlement programs do not fix problems they exacerbate problems. We need to change attitudes in order to change outcomes.

I Know What the Caged Bird Thinks of Me

Paul Lawrence Dunbar is the most famous writer from my neck of the woods. A brilliant writer, Dunbar's work is inspiring today and it made him the honored guest of the American president in his own day. His fame was well earned but his life was tragically short. As with a flame, those that burn brightest burn out quickest, Dunbar died early in life. He left behind an impressive body of work for one that died so young and his house in Dayton, Ohio is now a museum. Restored to its original splendor, the Paul Lawrence Dunbar house is a must see for local social studies students.

It was as a student teacher that I made my first visit to the Dunbar house. My Clinical Faculty, the teacher from whom I was learning to teach, and I carefully screened our students to decide who got to go on the field trip. There were grade requirements and behavioral requirements that the students had to meet in order to be allowed to go on the trip. Every student had to research Dunbar and choose one of his poems and write an opinion piece on how the work spoke to him. As with all requirements the research papers were meant to weed out the students that are too immature, too unrefined, and incapable of behaving with serene deference. It is a good thing that I did not have to meet the same requirements or I would not have been able to go on the trip.

While I am awed by the tenacity that it took for Dunbar to overcome the tremendous obstacles presented by the racism of his time, I do not feel that jocularity precludes respect. This is to say that I believe that it is OK for us to address the atrocities of our past with an air of humor. Laughing together at or differences and our struggles is a uniting endeavor. Some things are not funny but if we can find the humor in bad situations we go a long way toward healing those wounds of old.

My school was predominately African American and the trip reflected the racial makeup of the school rather well. Two teachers and one student were white, one student was Asian and the rest of the approximately one hundred students teachers and parent chaperones were African American. The Dunbar museum consists of his actual house and the two neighboring houses connected by passageways constructed for the museum. We three teachers each took one third of the students to a separate house of the museum because our group was far too large to stay together. As I walked with my group of thirty plus students into our first section of the museum I was surprised to see a beautiful African Macaw in an enormous brass cage. Knowing the longevity of such birds I wondered if it could possibly have been Dunbar's pet. I enquired about the bird at the very end of the tour and I was told the following tale.

When the Dunbar house was originally purchased to be made into a museum, an octogenarian lived across the street that had had Paul's mother as a babysitter in her youth. It was a good match for a fast friendship. A pleasant woman had first hand knowledge and stories about what life was like in Dunbar's time and neighborhood and the friendly museum staff gave company to a lonely, lovely, friendly woman. Time passed and the neighbor needed to take a trip to the hospital for a few days. As she had no other friends or relatives that lived in the area she asked that the museum curators watch her pet bird during her short stay. They agreed and sadly she passed away during that hospital visit. So now the Dunbar museum has a bird that does not necessarily belong there.

I began to usher my students past the bird and into a room with ten chairs in front of a large screened television on which a documentary about Dunbar's life was to play. The mood was reverent and somber as my Clinical Faculty had primed all of the students that there was to be no horseplay or other goofing around on this trip. I wanted to model the behavior that my clinical faculty expected from the students and I was doing a good job until the bird began yelling, "Craack-ER. CRAACK-er." As I was the only melanin deficient person in the room and the bird itself was an African Macaw, I got the idea that the bird was calling me out as an interloper on sacred ground. A bird calling me a cracker in a room full of blacks struck me as so funny that I began to grin. Coupling this with the fact that I was supposed to be somber was funnier still. I tried to stifle the laughter so it came out as a pained giggle.

All the while, the bird is calling me out, "Look at the 'Craack-ER.' Look at the 'CRAACK-er.' The 'Craack-ER' isn't being serious. The 'CRAACK-er' thinks this is all a joke." I was lost. I was supposed to supervise. I was supposed to put over thirty high schoolers into a room that was set up to hold ten and I was in the middle of a suppressed laughing fit that was not getting any better. The students started to notice actually asking me, "Are you alright, Mr. Callahan?" Apparently, I appeared to be in pain and as you know if you ever tried to stifle a laugh, I was in pain.

My laughing fit was compounded by the release of a mounting stress within my student teaching situation. My Clinical Faculty and I had a major personality clash. She thought that solemnity equaled professionalism. I thought, as I still think, that humor and laughter are legitimate aspects of human nature. We can laugh at things that strike us as funny without being disrespectful. The Clinical Faculty Student Teacher relationship is a horribly lopsided interaction. If a Clinical Faculty does not care to relinquish some power in the relationship to the Student Teacher then the experience is oppressive and dictatorial. I was not allowed to be myself in this particular teaching experience and the whole situation was so horrible, that I nearly dropped out or my teaching program. I tried to tough it out and be who she wanted me to be but I was not being true to myself and that made me a horrible teacher.

Sitting in a quiet corner of the museum I decided that I had had enough of hiding my true self and that regardless of the bad evaluation that I knew I would get from my Clinical Faculty, I began to laugh. I laughed and

I felt good, better than I had felt in over a month. I had taken back my identity, consequences be damned. If it was inappropriate to find humor in a bird yelling cracker at the lone white man in a room filled beyond capacity with African Americans, then I am inappropriate and I will always be inappropriate. I cannot take myself too seriously and I pity those that do take themselves too seriously. Dunbar knew why the caged bird sang and I found out why the caged bird sings once he has escaped his bondage. I laughed and laughed and although my Clinical Faculty was not in the room with me she found out that something changed the day that we visited the Dunbar house. I stopped trying to meet her impossible expectations and I went back to meeting my own.

Today I am an excellent teacher and I am so thankful that during my student teaching I was placed in a situation that stifled my own personality and my creativity. I learned from that experience that if someone does not want me to do a job my way then that person does not want me to do the job. If someone does not want me to do the job then I find a new job. Teaching is a serious job. It is, however, perfectly fine to be silly while you do a serious job. I am a consummate professional, one of the best teachers at my school. I am also a cut up, one who realizes that it is OK to have fun while you learn and to have fun while you live.

My Clinical Faculty did not like the new me, which was actually the old me but also the me that I tried to suppress to accommodate her expectations. She gave me a bad review just as I had expected. As a matter of fact I had to have a meeting at my college because of my low performance evaluation. There was much confusion because she was the second of three Clinical Faculties that I would have that year and her evaluation of my performance was diametrically opposed to the evaluation submitted by my first clinical faculty. In the meeting the college professors and counselors were quite candid with me. They said that over the years in their education program they had several students that were not suited to be teachers and I did not fit that mold. They were perplexed by the fact that in the nine years that the master of Education program was available I got the lowest evaluation in the programs history. I expected my student teaching to make me into a better teacher; my Clinical Faculty expected me to do her job for her while she sat at her desk listening to music. I scaled my clinical hours back to the required number of hours for my college program after my visit to the Dunbar house. (That was roughly half the number of hours my clinical faculty had me working up unto that point.) I stopped grading all of the homework and began grading just over half of what was assigned during my remaining student teaching. I began doing a reasonable amount of work and I regained the joy for teaching that I had lost.

My Clinical Faculty was upset that she had lost her personal assistant and I was upset that the incredible amount of extra work and initiative that I provided for her netted me a bad performance evaluation. My evaluation was so bad that it was the worst evaluation in the history of the master of Education program at my university. My evaluation was so bad that I had to have a meeting with the university's Education staff to see if I should be removed from the program. After I was assured by everyone present at the meeting—my Clinical

Faculty did not show up though she was invited—that they all knew that I had not earned the marks I was given by my Clinical Faculty, and that they would factor my final performance evaluation on my first and last performance evaluations only, I decided to let it go. I am not upset by what was done to me I will let it be her problem instead of mine. I do, however, mourn the missed opportunities to laugh during the bad time. I am sure that by now I have since made up for lost time and I still smile when I think of that trip to Dunbar's house. Paul, I wear the mask no more.

Mushfake

Spend a little time in prison and you will make a starling discovery. It is not like TV. Prison is a strange place filled with stress, anxiety, and the knowledge that violence can occur at any moment. The odd part about my prison experience is how quickly I became acclimated to the stressors of the environment. Everyone makes the adjustment to prison in his own way and deals with the unique blend of fear and intimidation in his own way. Many, usually the young guys, put on a display of bravado in order to impress upon the rest of us that their incarceration could not have been dealt to a meaner, more dangerous SOB. Using intimidation to deal with ones own fear seems to have mixed results among the population that employs this coping strategy. Many calm down, realizing that the grease received by the squeaky wheels in here, is applied in an area that no one ever wanted greased and that no one ever tells his homies about once he gets back out.

Yes, back out. Most of the incarcerated get back out onto the street to do as they will. This catch and release program is the reason for my own incarceration, which I serve eight hours a day, five days a week. I am a GED teacher in the prison. I serve my bit in installments but I am incarcerated just like the inmates. There are a number of things that occur in prison and nowhere else, at least nowhere that I have been. My relatively new exposure to prison life lets me notice things that the seasoned veteran takes for granted. Prison is a wonderful place. Of course, I am using wonderful to mean that it is full of wonders, curiosities, and not that the wonders are good by any stretch of the imagination. I wonder why so many things are done the way they are done. I wonder why anyone with reasonable command of his faculties would work in a prison. I wonder what the draw is of prison that so many prisoners come right back after being released.

The best place to start on the wonders of prison life is with the first time I set foot in a prison. That was the day I interviewed for the job I have now, GED teacher. I remember clearly being surprised at my lack of nervousness as I left my car, doors locked of course, in the parking lot and approached the only building on the compound with a section of wall and a door outside the fence. The Human Resources person that set up the interview gave me some pointers on what to bring in with me. She said, "Don't bring anything in that you can live without over the course of the interview. Pull the key that unlocks your car door off of the ring and lock the rest of your keys in your car." From this advice I had extrapolated the idea to leave my wallet in the car and to only bring in my driver license and social security card.

My first concern crept into my mind as I closed on the front door. How do I get in? I was sure someone would help me out with this but I did not want to appear confused, needy, or out of my element as I arrived for my interview knowing that first impressions are critical. Fortunately, when I was still some thirty odd yards from the building someone else approached the door. I witnessed the ritual and approached the door with renewed confidence. I was going to manage to get into the building without appearing flustered.

When I reached the door I pulled on the handle with an even amount of pressure and I waited for someone to push the button that unlocked the door. When that button was pushed, I discovered a part of the ritual that I had failed to notice earlier while observing from afar. The sound of the lock being remotely thrown was startlingly loud. I could actually feel the sound pass through my hand on the handle, up my arm, and out the back of my head. Thank God, I did not give a full bodied flinch, which is usual for me when I am startled, but I was then concerned that the prison worker at the front door was going to radio back to the interviewers, "Forget about this guy, he nearly peed his pants walking in the front door." I know now that I need not have worried. No sentence with less than three separate pieces of profanity has ever passed the lips of a Corrections Officer on duty. He might have said, "Forget about this #*@%!^& guy he nearly ?=!+ his #*@%!^& pants when I tripped the #*@%!^& lock on the door," but I guess he did not say that either.

I produced the proper paper work and identification. I cleared the metal detector and I was escorted from the front building, "A" building, past the "Key Control" building into "B" building. The first wonder that struck me inside the fence was the presence of bicycles. First, I could not imagine why the bikes were needed or who would be riding them. Next, I marveled at the lack of bike locks. I had never in my life seen a dozen or so bikes collected together in one spot without a single bike lock. I got a chuckle out of the fact that the very people for whom bike locks were invented, lived every day around bikes that no one feared would be stolen.

I interviewed for the job and went home having not seen a single prisoner and unsure as to whether or not my interviewers liked me. Five months later, I had all but forgotten my bizarre trip into the prison system when I was called to see if I was still interested in the job. I am now a GED teacher in prison.

Working in prison is a very specialized field. All specialized fields have jargon. Lawyers say things like *vis a vis*, et al, and my fee is payable upfront. Doctors say things like contusion, thrombosis, and no I am not receiving financial compensation for my preference of this one particular pharmaceutical company. Politicians say things like cloture, caucus, I am not a crook, I did not have sexual relations with that woman, and mission accomplished. Teachers say things like enrichment (worksheets), IEP (immediate excuse provider), and I do **not** only work nine months a year.

The field of rehabilitation and corrections is no exception when it comes to specialized jargon. Much of the jargon is replacing something's name with its initials as in CO, RIB, and IHS; which is to say Corrections Officer, Rules Infraction Board, and Institutional Health Services. Another source of jargon is the inmate population. Front street refers to bringing up a private matter in a public setting as in, "That CO chewed me out right on front street." Foxy is an "intoxicating" mixture of coffee and Kool-Aid meant to replace the alcohol that inmates no longer have access too. Inmates love to sit around drinking foxy, although they all would prefer hooch. I know of an inmate that went to a parole hearing and got flopped for a dime. Inmates beef with their cellies and avoid the yard dogs. Prison jargon is colorful indeed but one word, far and away above all others, succeeds in defining prison life and that word is mushfake.

As you would expect, prison life consists of very specific rules. There are rules about how inmates dress and how often they must attend to person hygiene. There are all sorts of rules to prison life and most inmates are not the type of people that are good at following rules. (Why else would they be in prison?) The most important rules in prison are what inmates can and cannot do and what they can and cannot have. Inmates cannot have tools, needles, or tattoo ink. Inmates cannot have items from their approved item list if those items have been altered in any way. This brings us to the term mushfake. Mushfake means any item that an inmate has altered to create an item that he is not allowed to have.

Every cell in prison contains mushfake coat hooks. Normally, the coat hooks are made from reshaped bedsprings but I have seen them made from wood and even cardboard. Cardboard is the hottest illegal commodity in prison. Necessity absolutely is the mother of invention. I would add that in prison cardboard is mother's medium of choice. I have seen a night stand with a chest of drawers so finely crafted that it would not have appeared out of place in a furniture store.

I have seen mushfake wrenches and screwdrivers to work on radios, fans, and televisions all of which become mushfake after the repair because they are no longer in their original condition. Mushfake TV remotes are popular items. I have seen simple mushfake remotes such as six feet of tightly rolled newspaper to push the buttons on the TV. Also, I have seen an old radio antenna with a pencil eraser on the end to prevent slippage on the TV buttons. I have seen incredibly complex TV remotes such as a row of wooden toggles glued over all of the buttons on the TV and connected to corresponding toggles glued to the wall over the bed by a taut system of string also running along the wall and turning two corners in the process. A toggle pulled on the wall would make the corresponding toggle on the TV press the button beneath it.

Knit hats are allowed but scarves and ski masks are not, but a small hole cut into a knit hat allows it to be pulled inside out. Once inside out the hat looks like a tube top and is functional as an instant scarf for cold winter days.

Mushfake is a way of life for prison inmates. They take what they are allowed to have and make what they want. Cassette players are stripped down into tattoo guns. Ashes are mixed with baby oil to make tattoo ink and there is no alcohol to swab an area prior to tattooing so infections run rampant. Mushfake defines prison better than any other word or idea. It is too bad that inmates have so much free time to sit around making illegal items. Items made from materials that are normally stolen either from other inmates or stolen from the prison itself which is stealing from me a taxpayer. As long as hands are allowed to idle, they will create hooch, shanks, and also create truly horrible things like bad poetry glorifying misdeeds, written with stolen pens on stolen paper. Instead, let us hand our inmates sledgehammers and allow them to make little rocks out of big rocks. Perhaps if prison life is unpleasant enough, people will not be so quick to do things that bring them back.

Accountability

The educational system in America is an absolute mess. So many college bound teens leave high school with an educational deficit that the fastest growing instructor need at America's institutions for higher learning is lower teaching. Kids are so pitifully unprepared that freshman English is required in all majors, just to make sure that students are able to read and write before they get into classes that teach them anything else. The result is the need for five to seven years of college to complete a bachelor's degree, a four-year degree. Colleges are in the business of higher education but they are still in business. The purpose of business is to make money; so spending seven years worth of tuition on a four-year degree is great for business. If we are to address the problem of educational deficits in America, we dare not look to colleges.

Another place that we cannot seek to remedy educational shortcomings is in the family. If I were to suggest that part of a parent's responsibility is educating a child, I would be making an insensitive statement at best and at worst I would be the reason that people are not succeeding. How can anyone achieve success if I stand in the way by suggesting that success starts at home? Parents do not need to bother with educating their children that is what school is for. If your child is not performing well in school it is everyone else's fault. No, we cannot look to an individual for having a hand in his own misfortune because nothing in this country is an individual's fault. If you do not believe me just look at the most lucrative business in America, tort lawyering. There is no business in America, not even that place with "always the low price," that brings in the yearly revenue as those champions of the little man.

Smokers are not responsible for choosing to smoke; fat people are not responsible for choosing to over eat and parents are surely not responsible for their children's education. How could lawyers get rich if people were responsible for their own actions?

I must focus. Today is the day for skewering a ridiculous program. I must save my qualms with the legal profession for a day when I have the time to write chapters rather than pages.

A problem with "No child left behind" is knowing ones place in the grand scheme of things. Who is better than the national government to create policy to fix problems on the district level? Certainly teachers, principals, school administrators, superintendents, and anyone else in a school district that could possibly know anything about the unique needs of the students in that district are not the ones to whom we should turn for input into what needs to be done to fix the problem. After all, what do teachers know about teaching? If they had any marketable skills, they would not have to teach for a living. No, we definitely need politicians to tell schools how to teach and what to teach. After all, we all know that politicians and the government in general are the most efficient and effective creators of policy and that a policy made on the national level could not possibly have an exception in a single school district in the entire United States.

Advocates of "No child left behind" are pushing a policy to get themselves elected. The idea of all American student reading and performing math at grade level within ten years sounds wonderful. Ideas that sound wonderful are the things that get politicians elected. It is not possible to have all people reading at grade level but it sounds wonderful. It could easily be said that my acknowledging that it is not possible is proof that I am abandoning the very students that need me most. Anyone with any sense at all knows that admitting realistic limitations is a long way from giving up. Setting realistic limits is in fact necessary to teach anyone anything. There is no way that everyone in America will ever perform at exactly the same level of proficiency no matter how "standardized" tests purport to be.

Our Declaration of Independence reads, "All men are created equal," but this does not mean everyone is truly created with equal faculties to read, write, learn, and create it simply means that all Americans have equal access to all freedoms and benefits of our nation. Equal access does not and cannot mean equal results from that access. Teachers teach. The good ones teach to each child's strength while strengthening each child's weaknesses. Oh yes, there are bad teachers. I had a few when I was in school and I have worked with a few. In my experience poor teachers have been a super minority. The problem of having a few bad teachers should not be the reason why schools are not allowed to set their own education plans. The national government is an extremely important aspect of America. It has, however, absolutely no business micromanaging education. "No child left behind" will fail. Great teachers will tire of nonsensical regulations and the educational field will lose them. Children that pass through school during this policy will be drilled with the limited scope of knowledge needed to pass proficiency tests and they will miss out on a full, well rounded education. Ten years from now all students will not read and perform math problems at grade level; however, ten years will put even the most fortunate of executive politicians safely out of office and, therefore, unaccountable for the failed policy. Oh, those crafty politicians.

Dollars and Sense

Taxes are too high. I hate that I have to pay so much in taxes and get so little of value in return for those dollars I pay. I cannot stand when schools beg for money and threats like, "If the levy does not pass, your children will have to find their own way to school next year," are incredibly off putting. I do not want to pay more taxes. I pay enough. It is not my fault that the government is a bloated bureaucracy filled with kick back taking, pork barrel spending, worthless law passing fat cats who put their own wants, needs, and desires ahead of the wants, needs, and desires of the voting public whom they are supposed to represent. The whole situation was a disgusting mess long before I was old enough to vote. I had no hand in causing the problem it should not be up to me to fix it.

Except, it is up to me to fix it. On a hot July fourth back in 1776 a couple of guys kicked together some grievances that they played no part in creating, but they did something about it anyway. They pulled together a less than mutually oriented group of people and formed a new nation with the goal of throwing off a bloated monarchy filled with kick back taking, pork barrel spending, worthless law passing fat cats who put their own wants, needs, and desires above the wants, needs, and desires of the people whose interests they should have been representing. I shall interject here that I do **not** advocate the overthrow of our government. It is the duty of every American citizen to overthrow our government if it becomes so laden with corruption that it is beyond redemption but America is not there yet.

Government in America is ailing. I do not believe that it is terminally ill even now but it is definitely in need of some doctoring. To fix the problem I would like to borrow a medical treatment that was extremely popular at the time our independence was declared. We must bleed the behemoth. We must lance the hundreds of boils that are poisoning democracy and we must let the bad blood run out.

I began with schools because education is the single most important expenditure of tax dollars. I do not want to hear schools beg for money because I already pay enough of my hard earned money into taxes. I do know, however, that schools desperately need more money so I will address two problems with a single scalpel stroke. Every government program on every level of government will have its tax allotment cut by ten percent. Paper pushers will be removed. Unnecessary jobs will be eliminated. All agencies will begin to be run as if they were private businesses where performance and bottom line results will be prized. I will scrap the current system where a mastery of filling out forms to give the impression that work has been done is more important than any work actually getting done. I will remove waste from all levels our government and it will create the kind of enterprise that will serve the people rather than serve itself. The primary function of most government agencies today is to ensure the perpetual need for that agency. I will remove self interest in government agencies and I will cut out the dead weight and the wasteful spending. Rather than pocket the revenue trimmed from the bureaucracy, I will immediately double the salary of every teacher in America. Just as quickly, I will hire new teachers at a ratio of one new teacher for every teacher currently in the educational system. With the additional revenue I will begin updating buildings and materials on an as needed basis. These simple steps will go a long way toward fixing our government and keeping it fixed.

The more education an individual has the less likely he is to go to prison. Education is inversely proportional to needing welfare assistance. Increased education decreases prejudice and hatred. More education makes you less likely to break the law and it makes you more likely to do volunteer work. Increased education increases your likelihood to vote. Most important to all of you bottom liners who do not give a flip about all of the heart warming information above, increased education increases your life long earning potential. Education turns tax burdens into taxpayers. Schools today are overcrowded with students and understaffed with teachers. The one expenditure that our society can least afford to do without is often the first cut when money gets tight.

Talking heads will say something along the lines of, "Well surprise of all surprises, a teacher thinks that doubling his own salary will somehow fix the education system." My response to such a bitterly mean spirited attack would be, "You're dammed right it will." I am an excellent teacher but it is a struggle to support my family on my teaching income alone. If times get any tougher, I will have to leave the most important job in America for better money elsewhere and that is a choice I would rather not have to make. If you make teaching a more desirable job by putting it on par with other occupations that require a master's degree, doubling salaries across the board will do that, you will open competition for the job and ultimately improve the quality of teachers. There are many people who would love to teach and who would make excellent teachers but the cost of the required education, weighed against the financial return of the job make it an impossibility.

I have seen great quantities of money wasted in an erroneous attempt to improve education through materials rather than through teachers. I did my student teaching in a district that was in financial crisis. There was a ground breaking for a new junior high school to replace the very building in which I was doing my student teaching. During the ceremony, the district's superintendent bragged in his speech about the $10.4 million state of the art building that would house the new junior high school. In the crowd of spectators were a number of the district's sixty-nine teachers that were fired the week before due to budget cuts. New buildings do not teach. Computers do not teach. New textbooks do not teach. The internet does not teach. Televisions do not teach. Standardized tests do not teach. People teach. If you want to fix a problem, you must present a real solution. Our children deserve more than a campaign slogan. Our country needs more than what we are getting for our tax dollars. Let us break the cycle of violence, the cycle of poverty, and the cycle of ignorance. A better-educated America is better for us all. Knowledge is power and teachers give it away. When we have a well-informed society we will fix the problems of our government with our collective voice, our vote.

Mental Health

Unlike a certain celebrity, I do not know the history of psychiatry, but I can commiserate. I had a problem with the idea that there is something wrong with you and you will never be right unless you take this cocktail of drugs. Also, the idea that people are broken but doctors can fix them with their prescription pad always made me think that some people are weak and they need a crutch to face life. Depression is all in your head. Suicidal people only lack strength of will. Anxiety disorder is no more than an introvert that needs to embrace his personality and come out of his shell on his own. Attention deficit hyperactivity disorder is nothing more than poor parenting.

These are all opinions that I held for the better part of my life. I refused to consider that a malady could exist, because I did not suffer from a mental illness. I believed that all but the most severe mental illnesses were merely a series of poor decisions. And I thought it was irresponsible bordering on criminal that doctors would take advantage of weak-minded people.

I have always been suspect of anyone peddling happiness from a bottle. I feel that the horrible side effects to many drugs sound infinitely worse than the benefit they claim to provide. I made a very human mistake. I assumed everyone was just like me. By definition most people are in the majority on all matters so we naturally tend to think that whatever is right for me is right for everyone. I do not need any drugs and neither does anyone else.

As I have met more people and encountered more of the variability of possible afflictions in life, I have had to adjust my worldview. I still do not think that medicines are needed but I realize that there is extraordinary benefit to be gained by many people in many situations. It is easy to disbelieve in chronic pain when you do not suffer it. It is easy to doubt the severity of another's depression when your own physiology plagues you with nothing more than the occasional blue moment. It is easy to assume that attention deficit is actually a discipline deficit when you have not spent untold hours with an otherwise well behaved, well adjusted child trying to impose a level of concentration on that child with sheer will power.

It is a question of privilege and the accident of birth. I was privileged to arrive malady free. I am not dyslexic, anemic, depressed, distressed, or overly impressed. The closest I come to anything defunct or deficient is the dominance of my sinister side and quite honestly lefties have not been persecuted during any part of my life. The nearest to ostracism that I have experienced is repeatedly answering the question, "Why do your scissors have green handles." I have the privilege of exceptional concentration, a jovial carefree outlook on life, and fully functional pain receptors. Who am I to say that others could not benefit from medical treatments just because I could not?

Do people deserve the chance to suppress symptoms that are negatively impacting the quality of their lives? Some will say no I must say yes. If pain medicine helps you enjoy a better quality of life, take it. If re-uptake inhibitors help you concentrate and allow you better success in school or life, good for you. If a pill can stabilize the balance of chemicals in your brain and pull you out of a debilitating depression, thank God you have a chance to enjoy life as much as I do. If you are a fellow that has more fame than sense, learn to smile and nod and remember that everyone loves it when you speak the words that someone else came up with.

Speeding Ticket

I got a speeding ticket a few days ago. I am not complaining because I actually was speeding. The problem I have is that I did not notice I was speeding. I was not watching my speed, I was paying attention to my surroundings and driving with the flow of traffic and not watching my speedometer. When I passed a State Trooper going in the opposite direction we made eye contact. At this point I glanced down at my speedometer. I saw that it was ten miles an hour above the posted speed limit and I said to my wife, "I just got a speeding ticket."

I slowed down to the posted speed limit and watched the reflection of the trooper make a u-turn in my rear view mirror. I did not stop right away because he did not have his lights on, yet I knew he was coming for me, I could see it in his face during our brief period of eye contact. I was traveling as the last car in a line of four, all of whom were going the same speed. Because of this, I clung to the hope that he had actually clocked one of the other cars and he would be passing me in pursuit of his true quarry. I knew I was lying to myself, I could read the truth of the matter in his face but the best part about hope is that it can fly into the face of mountains of fact and shout, "Pshaw! I refuse to believe." I was lying to myself and I knew it but it was nice to pretend.

The lights came on and I slowed down and drifted to the berm. The Trooper did not zoom past me, as I knew he would not, and he followed me to a stop at the side of the road. He came up to the passenger side of my car and when my wife rolled down the window he spoke in a very courteous manner, "I clocked you at sixty-eight and the speed limit through here is fifty-five. Where are you headed?" The question was asked in such a way that I knew the real question was, "Do you have a good reason to be speeding?"

I told the trooper that, "Yes, I am aware that I was speeding," and, "no, I do not have a good reason to have been speeding. My family and I are going into town for dinner." I once read an account by a police officer that he had been a cop for eleven years and in all of that time he had only had two people ever admit that yes, they were aware that they were speeding and no, they did not have a good excuse to be speeding. The officer was so flabbergasted by the honesty of these two drivers that he let both of them off with no ticket.

My trooper apparently saw no wisdom in such leniency. He made no comment on my refreshing honesty and he certainly showed no hesitancy in issuing me a citation. I am not upset over this incident because I was speeding and I understand why speed limits are enforced. I hold no illusions that public safety is the reason for speed limits for I know that countries with no speed limits have fewer per capita accidents than does the United States. I know that the true reason for speed limits and speeding tickets are the incredible revenue that they generate for law enforcement agencies.

I agree that one can drive too fast on certain types of roads, in certain conditions and in heavily populated areas. I do not believe that it is safe for anyone to drive any speed he wants any time and any place. What I do believe is that there are times when it is safe to drive in excess of the posted speed limit. In my own case it was much safer for me to have been speeding at the point when the trooper cited me than it was for me to drive in the manner that I did for the week or so immediately following the ticket. As I have previously mentioned I do not mind paying the speeding ticket. The police provide an invaluable service to society in general and to me specifically and they are expected to generate a certain percentage of there own budgets each year. My problem was with the way I was driving between the moment of my citation and the several days later that I paid my fine.

I certainly did not want to receive another ticket before I paid the fine for the one I had just received, so I became overly concerned about my speed. During normal driving I maintain a speed that feels comfortable and safe for the conditions of the moment, and I glance at the speedometer on the rarest of occasions and slow down as necessary. Driving around with the unpaid ticket in my pocket, however, my attention was held primarily by my speedometer and I gave only fleeting glances to the world outside of my car. Initially, I did not notice that my priorities had been dangerously reordered. Suddenly, while studying the slight tremor of my tachometer the thought comes into my head, "What am I doing?" All at once the frightening reality floods my mind. I had unconsciously replaced my priority of safety with the distraction of following the speed limit. I had unknowingly become a danger to myself, my fellow motorists, and any pedestrians that may have wandered near my distracted path. All of this danger to the community was a direct result of the fundraising practices of law enforcement agencies.

I am a huge supporter of peace officers. I respect and revere all of the men and women that risk there lives every day so that I may sit in relative safety and security and question everything. So thank you all for the opportunity to ask, "Is it an effective use of manpower requiring officers to spend a significant portion of their time raising their own monetary resources? Could the time that is spent fundraising with a RADAR gun be put to better use? Will writing this chapter increase the likelihood of my contributing to the fundraising efforts of law enforcement in the future?" Please know that this is not an effort to belittle the profession.

I can think of no tougher career choice than becoming a police officer. It takes a special breed of person to be entrusted with the option of deadly force and charged with the protection of the general population. Specifically, it takes an incredible human being to risk ones own life for those citizens who would have him/her publicly ridiculed, dishonored, and removed from service. As a teacher I find it easy to want to help people learn, even obstinate students that fight me at every step of the way. What I cannot fathom is how a cop can stand to serve and protect the bleeding hearts among us? Please, let us protect the rights of the criminals. I do not know how I could sleep at night knowing that a

dangerous thug was removed from the street in anything other than the kindest gentlest means necessary.
  I saw a distraught mother on television bemoaning the loss of her son and I can sympathize. If one of my children were to precede me in death it would be devastating no matter what that child had done to bring about that death. There was a public outcry over the death of this twenty-five year old "boy." A man came on the screen and demanded justice for the "boy" that was, "Shot down like a dog." The evil police were to blame for the senseless death of this fine upstanding young citizen of the United States.
  I have never in my life been gunned down like a dog. The zealot who made that statement would have pointed to the color of my skin as the reason for my safety. I have an alternate explanation as to why I have never been shot by the police. On the numerous occasions -unfortunately numerous is an accurate assessment- that the police have fallen in behind my car with lights flashing and sirens wailing I have made the decision that best suited my needs. I pulled my car to the side of the road and I politely followed all instructions that were given to me. You see every time a police officer approaches a car he is putting his life in jeopardy. I gave every officer absolutely no reason to fear for his safety and, therefore, no officer has ever had to take my life in order to protect himself.
  I have a different take on the relationship between police officers and the citizenry. An officer's job is to serve and to protect. Realize, when a cop pulls me over for speeding he is protecting the rest of you from my selfish choice to hurry. When an officer stops my car to inform me that it is against the law in the state of Ohio to

drive with one headlight out he is protecting me from the possibility—slim as it may be- that my other headlight might burn out before I replace the first lamp of my own accord, which would cause a dangerous situation. I am in a hurry to get home so that I can procrastinate on the chores that crop up in my life.

The police have many responsibilities when they relate to the public but it must be remembered that we as the American citizenry have responsibilities when dealing with police officers. Although I know that it feels wrong, be honest. If you were speeding you know it, so own it. You know how the drug pipe got into the car. And to the guy that served jury duty with me, *I* do not believe that you were wearing your seatbelt when the trooper spotted you and I wasn't even there. Be honest, be polite, and be glad that the officer is working hard to keep us safe.

Back to the twenty-five year old "boy," I would like to present my opinion as follows. If you peel away from a traffic stop and you lead the police in a high-speed chase, endangering the lives of the police officers themselves and the citizenry as a whole you deserve to be, "Shot down like a dog." If, at the end of your high-speed chase you ignore the officers' commands of, "Get on the ground" you deserve to be, "Shot down like a dog." If you are surround by police with their guns drawn and instead of heading their commands, you make a quick lunging grab into your jacket pocket and pull out a cell phone and you point the phone at the police in the same manner that they are pointing firearms at you, you had better expect to be, "Shot down like a dog."

I have nothing but respect for police officers. I could not do that job. I would shoot so many people. Let us please try to respect what the police are trying to do. We need to have someone protecting us. And maybe we could kick a couple of extra tax dollars to their budgets so they do not have to raise their own funds.

Religion

In my youth I went to church every Sunday. Neither of my parents went so I often questioned why I had to go. My mother's response invariably was, "I had to go when I was a young so you kids [my sisters and I] will go to church." While this response stopped my questioning, I would never have badgered my parents, it did not answer the question to my satisfaction. It was a question I often asked myself back when I had to go to church and it is a question I continue to ask myself today now that no one can force me to attend church.

My mother's insistence that I go to church when she did not attend puzzled me. Why would it be important for me to go if it was not important for my parents to go? It seemed to contradict everything that they were teaching at the church. Yet, I am glad Mom made me go. I was exposed to a way of thinking that I never would have known without church. Also, since my parents did not go to church, I did not feel compelled to blindly believe everything I was taught. I had what may be a very unique opportunity in my religious education. I had access to ideas that non-church-going kids did not. I also had the opportunity to evaluate the information provided and then use my own judgment to assess its validity, which kids with religious parents do not have. Before I go any further, I will put here that I attended a protestant Christian church. All Christianity that is not Catholicism is technically protestant regardless of how each denomination attempts to distinguish itself from the other denominations. I want this clear because I am not a theology scholar, although you do not need to be a scholar to hold opinions about religion. I went to one specific type of protestant Christian church and, therefore, I cannot speak with much authority on other religions but I know enough about them to hold an opinion.

Given the freedom to decide for myself about religion, I began questioning my beliefs in my teens when I began inwardly questioning all aspects of my world. I came to a point where I noticed a common theme to most religions. That common theme can be best summed up in, "We are right, and everyone else is wrong. We have the only path to God and everyone else is going to hell." My church was no exception to this theme and it was the part of church that I could not buy into. As it turned out, I had no problems accepting miracles and God's good grace but that elitism seemed to contradict the point of religion. For me, there had to be more to my religious affiliation than just a ticket into heaven. I began with the most basic question. It turned out to be the most difficult, "Is there really a God?"

Just because I had the freedom to draw my own conclusions did not mean that I did not ask others for their thoughts. I figured that if someone else had answered religion questions to my satisfaction that would be less work for me. So, I asked everyone that I could, "Why do you believe in God?"

To my dismay, yet not to my surprise, everyone I asked gave some variation of one of two responses. The most common response to the question was the one I expected, "Because the Bible says so." The problem with this response is called circular reasoning, something I understood in my teens although I did not know the phrase. People believe that the Bible is true because it is the word of God and it must be true and perfect because God is perfect. These same people believe in God because the Bible says to. You cannot use the book that draws its validity from God as your proof of God. This is like saying, "I believe my Congressman does not lie because he wrote me a letter that reads, 'I do not lie.' And I believe that the letter is true because of my belief that he does not lie so the letter must be true." We all know that your Congressman lies just like my Congressman lies. This logic does not hold up.

To my horror, the only other response given as the reason that people believe in God is some variation of, "Because the preacher tells me I should." I cannot even number all of the flaws in this reasoning. My concern is the blind faith in church people. Some people believe in God blindly, which is OK because if God does exist, He will not take advantage of that faith and trust. While I believe that most church people try to be good, honest, and just; they are only people and people are capable of evil, lies, and pain. Besides the capacity that good people have for doing bad things, there are truly despicable people who will gladly use the faith and brotherhood of religion to do terrible things to unsuspecting believers. I am always afraid for churchgoers. As they believe in the goodness and rightness of God, they begin to believe in the goodness and rightness of the people that teach them about God. This attitude makes the Bible's metaphor of churchgoers as sheep a particularly accurate depiction. Beware gentle sheep you know not what wolves walk among you. Go ahead and put your faith in God but please keep a wary eye on your fellow followers.

So, I found that no one could help me in my search for whether or not God really exists. Being a reasonably bright teen I realized that even if God did not exist there would be no harm in believing in Him when you die; however, if He does exist you would be in a world of hurt, at the time of your death, if you did not believe. This realization still was not good enough for me, however, because it was and still is my opinion that if God does exist, He would not be happy that I believed in him, "Just in case."

So, after much thought and much soul searching I came to my decision about God. I believe in God. Although my reason for belief may not be good enough for everyone, it suits me perfectly. I believe in God because I want Him to be real. I want there to be someone looking out for me. I want there to be a reason for this crazy progression of happenings we call life. I want that caring, nurturing, forgiving, understanding God that I read about in the Bible to be real. I want God to be real so I believe He is real. I want there to be purpose to life so I believe in God.

Now that I had the big question answered, to my own satisfaction if to no one else's, I had the next most important decision to make. Which religion is right? My understanding of Protestant Christian belief is, "We are right and everyone else is wrong and they will all burn in hell if they do not adopt our beliefs about religion." Perhaps I am making too large of an assumption here but I suspect that this is a common theme among the other religions as well. How else can we explain holy wars and killing for religion if it is not attempting to impress eternal salvation upon the heathen hordes?

This concept does not jibe well with a compassionate, understanding God. I just can not see a benevolent divine creator deciding that being honest, loyal, kind, helpful, respectful, generous, caring, and loving is all well and good but if you do not package these traits into the correct religious affiliation, you are still worthless and will burn in hell. Religion should be inclusive and accepting not exclusive and judgmental. Religion should be the pursuit of harmony and serenity not the pursuit of money and power. Religion should be fulfilling enough that we raise others up with our understanding not hold them down with our superiority. Religion should bring us together not drive us apart. Religion is a collection of positive ideas and beliefs that have been distorted and corrupted by the human drives of greed, jealously, and vanity.

I am endlessly amazed by the pride, jealousy, and spite that people can muster in defense of their personally chosen religions. People belittle others with the certainty that they know, absolutely know, that their interpretation of the Bible is true and correct. "The Bible is very clear, you just don't want to hear what is has to say," I overheard a "reverend" proclaim to someone that disagreed with him. To revere means to show deference but this man never deferred to any power greater than his own vast knowledge and superior understanding. Pride is one of the seven deadly sins and it is the bane of the existence of the vast majority of the religious people I know. People love to gloat and flaunting one's religion as the one true way is the ultimate vanity.

From "An eye for an eye," and "Turn the other cheek," to "Ingest no blood" and "This is my body and my blood," the Bible is anything but very clear. Even if the Bible was divinely inspired it was written by man and subject to the mistakes of sinful pride, jealousy, and certainty as everything else that we have a hand in. If you do not believe the Bible is subject to human error just look at the apocrypha. A group of men read the Bible and decided among themselves which books should be retained as the complete Bible and which books should be removed. Revelations just barely made the cut. Several books of the original Bible were not so lucky. My point is that either the apocrypha were not truly part of the Bible and, therefore, the authenticity of all of the Bible books are called into question or the apocrypha are real books of the Bible and we are using a text that has been altered for worldly reasons rather than for divine understanding. Either way, the Bible was wrong or it is wrong now and it is certainly subject to interpretation and it is not clear and obvious.

In the history of humanity, more wars have been fought over religion than all of the other reasons for war combined. This fact alone has made organized religion a target of mine for years. Be good to one another is a prevailing theme among all of the religions I have looked into yet every religion has had people who saw fit to kill other people in the name of their religion and their God. How the leap is made from, "Turn the other cheek," to "Death to the infidel," is beyond me.

Religions were created to explain the world around us. Something that most people do not want to accept is that every mythology was once a primary religion and every primary religion was once a cult. The mythologies began as a way to explain occurrences in nature. People depended on rain for their crops and for survival. When it did not rain and people started to die it was because the gods were angry and they were punishing the people. The worship of natural phenomenon was a predictable result of the deadly consequences of not understanding what we today call earth science.

Humans can ask why and religion attempts to answer why. An idea of an afterlife evolved from the idea of gods and otherworldly planes of existence. First, there was only one place that all people went to when they died. Then people decided that it made more sense that what you do while you are alive should influence what happens to you after you die. At that point it was decided that people who attended certain religious services, and more importantly paid their offerings to the church, could look forward to a better afterlife than everyone else. People were drawn to religion on this point. The squalor and despair of life could be better tolerated if bliss after death could somehow be guaranteed.

It did not take long for people to find problems with buying one's way into a better afterlife. Wicked people, who were wealthy enough to afford the church's price, would have a better afterlife than virtuous people that happened to be poor. A merit system was then added to the requirements for entry into the preferable afterlife. In competition for the revenue of members, religions began claiming to have the exclusive formula for entry into the preferred afterlife. It was around these philosophies that the cults of modern day religions were formed. Faced with persecution, violence, and death cult members found strength in their religions and solace in their congregations. It becomes the mission of every member of a religion to convert outsiders to the truth. Large congregations ensure the financial well being of the church, in return the church ensures entry into the Elysian Fields, Heaven, Nirvana, or whatever other name the church gives to the preferred afterlife.

In a clumsy, unenlightened manner I have brought us from the beginnings of religion to the practices of the present day. My obvious wealth of knowledge of the progression of religion to date makes me an authority to project the direction religion will take in the future. Religion has always been used to give people a better understanding of the world around them. The thunder god was angry and cast his lightening bolts to the ground in his rage. Today, we use science to explain the world around us. I see some kind of science worship for the people of the future. Not necessarily the science churches of today but some kind religion that fully incorporates the laws and principles or the modern day sciences will be the primary religion of the future. I am not the only one that thinks so. Religious people would not be pushing their pseudo-science Intelligent Design if they did not realize the shifting of trust from their religious certainty of indisputable doctrine toward the trial and error open mindedness of the scientific method. Intelligent Design was created to explain a preconceived notion and will, therefore, never be confused with science but it is an attempt to slow the transition from the primary religions of today to the religions of the future. God, Allah, and Yahweh will one day be studied with Jove, Thor, and Zeus. If that day comes in my lifetime, I will retain my own faith in God and my skepticism in humanity.

Save the Planet

Although the fervor has died down quite a bit since the eighties, there seems to be a prevailing sentiment that the planet needs us to save it. People have seen the error of their ways and now we must save the planet from deforestation, from fossil fuel emissions, from CFC's, from ozone depletion, from litter, and from environmental terrorism just to name a few. The idea goes that if we do not stop dumping pollution into the environment, we are going to destroy the planet. If we do not wake up and face the irresponsible indifference with which we regard the environment the earth is going to go the way of the Tyrannosaurus Rex, the Dodo bird, and thankfully the Macarena. This, of course, is pure nonsense.

Any "pollutant" that we put into the environment came from the environment; it belongs there. We will not destroy the planet by polluting it. Earth is resilient. It can take a whole lot more punishment than any that we can conceivably dole out, so go ahead and toss a bag of fast food trash out of your car window. Go ahead and drain the oil from your engine right onto the ground. You will not hurt the earth. You do not have to worry about saving the planet it will not be destroyed by any damage we do to it. It can, however, be made far too toxic to continue to sustain human life.

Save the planet is a ridiculous concept. People will do very little to effect the overall well being of our planet, the most we ever succeed in doing is to change the form of the substances that we pull from the environment. When you look at it on a global scale, the amount of time that the materials that we change stay changed is minute. I used to hear that plastic will last forever and that it will never be broken down by the environment, now I know that museums with original space exploration suits have trouble keeping their displays clean and dusted because the plastic parts of the suits are already beginning to degrade less than forty years after they were made. No, we cannot hurt the planet but we can and we will make it uninhabitable for ourselves if we do not change our ways. The problem arises when we try to decide what to fix. Where can we make positive changes for our habitat without putting too much strain on our comfortable lifestyle?

Why, we can make changes in the Third World of course. Incidentally, we can no longer call them the Third World we must call them LDC's which stands for Less Developed Countries, which defines their existence as it compares to and falls short of ours, which sounds much more derogatory than Third World to me. We must be diplomatic in the way that we refer to the Third World, which in turn allows us to tell them what to do with their natural resources. Do not cut down the rainforest in order to bring agriculture to your impoverished area providing food for the hungry and jobs for the jobless.

Cutting down the rainforest will lead to global warming and it will deplete our oxygen supply. It is a good thing we in the First World found this out after we cut down all of our own forests and created the space we need for our own economic expansion but now that we know how important forests are in the delicate web of life it would be irresponsible for you countries of the Third World to destroy yours and put yourself on a level playing field with us.

The rainforest has little to do with global warming except that plants filter greenhouse gases, some of the pollutants we nations of the First World dump into the environment, out of the air. We want those savages to remain backward so that we can maintain our lifestyles for as long as possible. As I sit writing this passage, in a spot that was dense forest 200 years ago, I marvel at the, "Do as I say not as I do" parenting that the United States passes for foreign policy. Learn from the errors of our past, Third World. It is your responsibility to the global community to preserve the remaining forests of the world. We are so sorry that this is not a paid position per se but there are all types of compensations when we speak of community services. You will all have the satisfaction of being the keepers of the forest and the saviors of our planet and our way of life. Now we realize that you may not find our current way of life to be worthy of saving but that is just because you are taking the word "our" as to include your way of life. You can never think that we are in any way including you in any possible benefits of a desired outcome. Ever.

So, thank you in advance for your cooperation in this matter. We look forward to working with you in the resolution of this matter. Of course, by "working with you" we mean you will be doing the work and we will be reaping the benefits. Again, Thank you.

The Lesson of Lemmings

Lemmings are rodents native to Scotland. Rodents are generally prey animals; which means carnivorous, meat eating, animals kill and eat them. Many people are not comfortable with the food chain and the life cycle but understand that prey animals need predators to keep their population under control.

An example of this need for population control in the state of Ohio is the white-tailed deer. Nature provided predators to keep the deer population within a range that is acceptable for the available food and territory. These predators include wolves, coyotes, cougars, and bears. Unfortunately, people do not like to share our space with apex predators so the large predators were exterminated in order to provide space for human expansion and ultimately to fulfill our Manifest Destiny.

It may seem like a good thing for the deer to remove the animals that kill and eat them but this is a faulty form of logic common to people that put the needs of an individual above the needs of the community. Deer breed so successfully that their population outpaces their resources and habitat. The deer population reaches and then passes a point known as critical mass, which is the maximum population density that an area can support. Once critical mass is passed, starvation sets in. There is no longer enough food so all of the deer in a population suffer malnourishment. The weakest deer of the population either die of starvation or they catch a disease that their undernourished immune systems cannot handle and they die from the disease. Eventually, the population drops back below critical mass and the surviving deer can flourish once again, building their strength in order to reproduce past the point of critical mass and starting the cycle over again.

While being killed and eaten is bad for the deer that it happens to, it is good for the deer population as a whole. The sacrifice of a few is necessary for the well being of society. This idea brings us back to Lemmings.

Lemmings live in an area where they have no natural predators. With our knowledge of the feast and famine cycle of the white tailed deer we could expect some similar cycle to transpire within the lemming population. We could expect such a cycle only if we did not know the one aspect of lemmings that makes the rodents famous.

Lemmings have adapted a behavior unheard of in any other species in the natural world. As the population of lemmings approaches critical mass rather than begin the cycle of starvation, disease, death, and a slow rebound; lemmings commit mass suicide. Through cues not even vaguely understood, a mass of the lemming population will break off of the lemming community and it will dive off of the Scottish cliffs into the ocean. While many white-tailed deer throw themselves in front of moving vehicles each year, these isolated examples of self-sacrifice do not compare to the lemming ideal.

This mass suicide, while bad for the individuals that plunge to their deaths, is good for the lemming population as a whole. The lesson we should learn from the lemmings is that we individual citizens can and should make personal sacrifices from time to time for the betterment of mankind as a whole.

This is not to say that mass suicide will in any way benefit our society. Please do not kill yourself. You are much more useful to mankind alive than dead. Even if your only useful contribution in life is to buy my next book, that is enough for me so hang in there. The point is we can all live better more meaningful lives by making small sacrifices in our own lives in order to improve the lives of others.

Truck drivers are a perfect example of where to start. Without over the road truck drivers, the ease and convenience of American life as we know it would stop. The banana I ate this morning is not native to Ohio. If it were not for truck drivers I would have had to have eaten something less tasty. I truly appreciate the contribution that truck drivers make to American life in general and to my life in particular. Thank you for a job well done. There is, however, one question that I feel I need to ask. If you are only going to drive one mile an hour faster than the trucker in front of you, do you really need around him? Look, I am sorry that you are not allowed to drive as fast in your truck as I am allowed to drive in my car, but your speed limit is not my fault. So please discontinue forcing me to drive the double nickel for the four and a half miles it takes you to get around pokey. I feel better already getting that one off my chest and this small sacrifice will greatly benefit society as a whole.

While I am on the driving soapbox I want to add a few more points. If you can remember a time when there were no cars, it is time for you to stop driving yours. Also, the stick on the side of the steering column that makes the green arrows on your dashboard blink is there to let other motorists know your intentions so use it. Do us all a huge favor, hang up and drive, put down the sandwich and drive, leave the radio alone and drive. Finally, the cop that has someone pulled over is not going to dart back into traffic to catch a speeder, he already has one so lay off the breaks. Also, if you see any suicidal deer flash us a warning with your headlights. Thank you.

This would be a great lesson to learn from lemmings. Everything fits so neatly together. Self-sacrifice for the good of the community is a beautiful thing. However, the true lesson of lemmings is not to believe everything you read. You see lemmings do not have a culling instinct where a section splits off from the community and commits mass suicide to prevent the disease and death associated with surpassing critical mass. The entire story is only a legend with no basis in actual fact.

The reason why I bring it up at all is that this story was taught to me in grade school as if it were fact. I was hurt and angry when I found out the truth. Did my teacher lie to me to prove how foolish I was? No, this was not the case at all. My teacher simply taught me what was taught to him. As a matter of fact I have recently discovered an old science textbook that presents this story as if it were fact. People did not know that the story was only a legend so it was presented as fact.

Along with not believing everything we read lemmings should teach us not to be afraid to admit when we are wrong. Science as a course of study collectively said, "Oops, we were sure wrong about that one. We hope it doesn't happen again but we are pretty sure it will." There is no shame in being wrong. The only real shame is not being able to admit you are wrong. It is neither manly nor macho to stubbornly stick to an erroneous thought process in the face of overwhelming evidence to the contrary. Being able to admit our mistakes is the only way to advance in our society. So, admit you are wrong, get your vehicle out of my way, and know that these small sacrifices will greatly benefit society.

Work

Originally, I wanted to use my favorite quote from my Uncle Wayne to title this chapter. I decided later to create a list of universal truths as defined by members of my family and me. I agree whole heartedly with Wayne's sentiment because, "Anyone who says, 'Hard work never hurt anybody' never did any."

Back in my undergraduate college days discussing life-altering decisions during a political theory class my professor asked me, "Why did you come to college?" Pointing first to my temple and then to my bicep I answered, "Because it is easier to work with this than it is to work with this." Pointing to his own bicep the professor replied, "True, but sometimes it is more fun to work with this." He went on to say, "There is nothing I enjoy more than working in my garden."

My professor was right. Quite often, physical labor is more fun than intellectual pursuits. I, myself, enjoy splitting firewood. The part that my professor overlooked is that his joy in gardening, just like my joy in chopping wood, is based at least partially in the fact that we do not have to do it. My professor loves to work in his garden because he can work it when he wants to work it and he can leave it when he wants to leave it. If the livelihood of his family depended upon him working sun up to sun down six or seven days a week picking in a farmers field, I guarantee he would see the difference between hard work and mind work. Chopping wood would certainly lose its appeal to me if I had to do it for a living. Thankfully, I was afforded the opportunity to go to college so that I may work with my mind in order to earn my living and I can use physical activity as a leisure activity.

My grandfather did hard physical labor his entire life. His father had gone to school and often lamented that it had done him no good so Sam, Grandpa, did not need to go. At the age of eight, Grandpa started working. He would fill a coal bucket with stones and dump them into a pile out of the way. When he started this job, he could only fill the bucket three quarters of the way because he was not strong enough to lift the bucket when it was filled to the top. His work was hard and it did not get any easier as he got older.

Grandpa worked for a coal mining company in Appalachia Tennessee. He worked long hours seven days a week and still did not earn enough to support his family so he moved with his brother-in-law Jess, up to Ohio because he was told that money grew on trees up this way. When he got to Ohio, Grandpa failed to find the money tree but he did find a job. He began working in a foundry that made aluminum and cast iron cookware. Grandpa's job was to shake the pots and pans out of the molds as they came out of the furnace. They had to be shaken out immediately because if they cooled too long they would stick to the mold and it would be impossible to remove them.

I cannot even begin to imagine the pain and hardship Grandpa went through to provide for his family but I can appreciate what he did and now that I have kids of my own I know exactly why he did it. He said to me once, "John, I had to work my whole life. I wasn't allowed to go to school and make something of myself. So, I decided that if I every had any kids of my own, every one of them would finish school."

Grandpa worked hard, harder than I want to imagine, so his kids could have an easier life than he had. True to his word, all three of Grandpa's sons graduated high school. My dad took the opportunity he was given and made a family of his own.

When compared to Grandpa's life, Dad did have an easier "row to hoe," but this is not to suggest that Dad's life was easy and care free. Dad has a high school education, which has opened doors for him that were closed to his father but that is not to say he missed out on work, real work, physical labor.

Dad worked long hard hours to support his family; the asphalt business is very demanding. I remember waking up to get ready for school in the morning and Dad had already left for work. More times than were healthy for him he would return home from work after I had already gone to bed. Summer was a long stretch of twelve to sixteen hour days with a healthy dose of mandatory Saturdays thrown in for good measure. Amazingly, autumn brought even longer workdays and many seven-day workweeks in an attempt to finish projects before winter hit. Winter brought a reprieve from the insanity and a return to the forty-hour workweek when only equipment maintenance was needed.

Dad worked hard but he also had the capacity to advance. Today he still works pretty crazy hours but he now managers the laborers rather than laboring himself, although he is still required to swing a pickax or jump on a front-end loader from time to time when the need arises. Much like his own father, my father worked hard to give me an easier "row to hoe" than his own. I appreciate the sacrifices that Dad made for my sisters and me.

I was the first person in my family to go to college. I once asked my dad why he never went to college being that he is definitely smart enough for post-secondary study. His answer has stuck with me and I feel that this answer was a disservice to my father by his teachers, his school administrators, and his guidance counselors. He told me, "I never knew it was a possibility for me. Being the son of a couple of illiterate hillbillies just graduating high school seemed like an incredible accomplishment." I understand this sentiment but someone at his high school should have seen within him the ability to go beyond and to make the idea of college seem accessible. His school dropped the ball when they handed him a diploma, shook his hand and forgot about him. Dad does not begrudge his life but I thought I noticed the glimmer of missed opportunity cross his face when I posed the question. It is because of this exchange that I ask every child I meet if they plan to go to college. College is not for everyone but it should be up to the individual to weigh the merits of college and to see whether or not it fits into their idea of what direction their life will take.

I do not want to leave my mom out here. She too worked hard to make me who I am today. My sisters and I were my mom's work; nearly unheard of in this day and age she was a homemaker. Mom instilled many traits into me that I thank her for. She taught me respect for rules and for other people. She gave me discipline when I needed it and always listened to my side of the story before providing that discipline. Mom and Dad gave me the tools I would need to become a happy and well-adjusted man.

Living the part of my own life where it is now my turn to work, I look back on the sacrifices that were made by the people dear to me that gave me the opportunities that I have today. I am thankful that I do not have to work with the incredible physical demands or the insane number of hours that my father and grandfather worked. I am thankful that I had so many people that cared about me that they gave their all so that I might succeed. Now that I have a wife and kids of my own, I understand their commitment.

Although my work is not physically demanding I too am a hard worker. I was raised with an emphasis on a strong work ethic, but this is not the only reason I work so hard. I could give just enough effort to do an acceptable job at work but I strive to be the best I can be as a way of saying thank you to my parents and grandparents and my whole family for all of their love and support. I want to be the example for my own children that my parents were for me. I want to raise the quality of life for my children just as my own quality of life was raised. I want every opportunity for my children so I work hard to create opportunity for myself.

President

I will be the most despised president of recent history. My effigy will be burned from sea to shining sea and no one will elect me to a second term. My four-year term as president, assuming that I escape the crosshairs of an assassin's scope, will go down in history as having the lowest approval rating ever. I can assure you that voters and businesses alike will be outraged by my lack of attention to the special interests of wealthy and powerful individuals.

I will not lie for your vote. I will not tell you that I will solve all of the problems of the world. I will not cut taxes. I will not increase spending and I will not do any of the popular things that presidents do for purposes of being re-elected because ultimately they weaken our country.

Like Ross Perot, I agree that the federal deficit is the single most important issue that must be addressed in the United States of America. Unlike Perot, I am tall enough to be elected president. So, I will take my six foot plus frame, my winning smile, my peculiar looks that could only be described as handsome by a myopic, and my hard edged, determined personality and win the presidency.

As I have already mentioned, all government spending will be cut across the board by ten percent and the proceeds will be added to the budget of the department of education. Incidentally, the central office of the department of education will also be cut by ten percent and all funds will be distributed to the schools.

The main fix to all of the problems in America will be so unpopular that it will spark those effigy burnings. I will raise the money for the paying down of the deficit by raising the tax on gasoline and other petroleum products. I will raise the price of gasoline to ten dollars a gallon.

Before you grab the Lynch rope, listen to all of the problems that this move will fix. Also, realize that lawmakers never consider the complete ramifications of the policies they enact. I, however, have looked into the possible effects of my remedy and except for the snipers posted at my every stop; all of the outcomes are great.

The first benefit from ten dollar a gallon gasoline will be the drop in emissions from the stop of unnecessary car trips. When people stop taking drives just for the sake of driving, when people begin car-pooling for similar drive routes our environment will benefit. A second benefit to the environment will be the more careful handling of expensive gasoline. When the Exxon Valdez ruptured, I was amazed by the story that all of the pollution spilled into the environment from that accident was less than one third of the total amount of gasoline spilled by overfilling our tanks at the gas pumps in a typical year in America. Certainly, the new pumps that cut off before the tank is completely filled have helped stop the polluting of the environment but at ten dollars a gallon I would no longer allow that occasional drop from the hose to hit the ground. Finally, consumers would demand more fuel-efficient cars and that would definitely improve the environment. I have read that the most fuel-efficient cars on the road today are only 15% efficient against the potential energy that can be derived from gasoline. This means that the automobile technology could quadruple in efficiency without even approaching the limit of gasoline's potential. This would bring the relative expense of fuel down to the prices of today.

A second benefit from increasing gas prices is the increase of exercise for our morbidly obese country. I will admit that I once lived three blocks from grocery store and I drove to that store more often than I walked to it. I dare say that I am not the only one that takes unnecessary drives in my car. I have seen more than one person drive his garbage to the end of his driveway. We will walk or bicycle to places that we once drove because we will weigh the inconvenience against the cost and we will choose the exercise for the sake of economy.

A third benefit to increasing the price of gas will be strengthening the ties of the community. I have lived in places where I did not even know my neighbors' names but I would drive up to thirty minutes to hang out with people I already knew. As I am staying near my house and my neighborhood, I will get to know the people I live near and I will become part of that community and we will work together toward our common goals. Also, the prohibitive cost of gasoline will make the prices at the super amazing outlet stores less appealing and we will see the return of the local mom and pop general store.

Seeing our neighbors at the store and at the other community functions will return us to an idealized America that had never heard of the metric system.

A final benefit that huge gas prices would bring to America is that it would sever our dependence on petroleum from questionable source countries. Personally, I would hate to pay ten dollars a gallon for gas but it would be worth it to me if I could know that the crude oil that makes my gasoline was not funding organizations that want to kill me. Right now, American foreign policy bans trade with countries that harbor terrorists unless those countries have oil. We are so dependent on oil that we are willing to fund efforts to destroy our society in order to get our fix. With all of our strength and influence on the international stage we are like a twitchy, back peddling junky when we address the atrocities that are allowed to occur in our supplier countries.

We need a return to our greatness. We were a country that would stand together against oppression and degradation. Now we are gluttonous, individuals who cannot be bothered by the problems of others. As long as I have my car and I can go where I want when I want, everyone else needs to find his own way. President Callahan will be hated but he will put aside his personal ambitions to do what is right for the country. Let us pay down the deficit, wean ourselves from our addiction, and strengthen our communities.

Contempt of Court

There is nothing I love more than the majestic beauty and the regal tradition of the American courtroom. There is a pervasive awe inspired by the dignified reverence in the proceedings. I love the heraldry. I love the lofty feel of importance. I love the deference shown to the honourable judge. And if you believe that I would love to show you a bridge that is affordably priced and sure to be a quick sell.

Like most Americans, I have disdain for anything that smacks of nobility. When I am in a courtroom and I am required to rise and to acknowledge the excellence and grandeur of the honourable judge, I cannot help but wonder why this elitism was allowed to remain when King George III was cast off a couple of hundred years ago. Robbing me of my right to contempt negates the legitimacy of the entire legal system. America is different. We do not dip the American flag in deference to the royalty of the host country during the Olympics. We do not contribute American soldiers to the United Nations like other members because our soldiers will not be told what to do by non-American commanders. We accept the huddled masses with greater regularity than any other developed world power. We sing our national anthem before sporting events. We believe that all men are created equal. Why do we put up with the self-important arrogance of our legal system?

I do not mean to insinuate that all judges are bad. There are plenty of good people in the judiciary working to make America better and keep America great. The grand standing that we are forced to endure upon threatened penalty of contempt of court sours me on even the purest of legal souls. My right to contempt is inseparable from my pursuit of happiness. Lovers of America are a strict minority in our courtrooms and we need to change that.

"Who do you think you are?" telling me that I may not hold your proceedings in contempt. You are telling me from jump-street that you want me to lie to you. This is the basic flaw of our legal system. The system is not interested in finding the truth. The system is not interested in actual guilt or innocence. The whole process is a dog and pony show where each side is attempting to conjure an effect from thin air. It is the job of the prosecutor to do everything in his power to convict you regardless of whether or not you did it. It is the job of the defense attorney to prevent your conviction regardless of your guilt or innocence.

Evidence is suppressed, which apparently means legally hiding facts that go against the lie that the lawyer is trying to make prevail. Once a case is begun a prosecutor will work to suppress anything that suggests the guy he is pinning the blame on had nothing to do with the crime. People are released from prison who were wrongfully convicted all of the time. Of course, prosecutors are not the only ones trying to suppress evidence. I just heard a news report of a case before the Supreme Court where a defense attorney wanted to throw out the **fact** that his client still had crack in his pocket when police executed a search warrant because the cops did not knock before entering the home. Am I the only one disgusted by this? These types of occurrences are not the justice I was taught to believe in as the American way. We, you and I, allow this crap to continue. As long as I seethe about it but stand idle, this mockery of the rights that I hold dear will proceed. It is easier to just go with the flow. I did not create the problem so it is not my job to fix it. John Q. Public must get more than pissed off we must get active.

Lawyers have told me they are, "Just doing my job," but that is the most shameful phrase ever uttered. "I'm just doing my job," says to me, "Yes, I know it is wrong but this is the way it is done and I just want to get home after a long day of work and forget about my job for a while." How can anyone, lawyer or otherwise, live with himself with this philosophy? Lawyers make their livings off of human misery. A friend of mine once told me that, "All judges are just bad lawyers," because a lawyer can make so much more money than a judge can, no one would be a judge if he was any good at selling his lies as a lawyer. My friend was making a joke and like all really funny jokes it was just a little too close to the truth to be comfortably contemplated. In my experience, I have never met a good lawyer. I am sure that there are plenty who enter the profession looking to restore its honor but the corruption of the system either wears away the ideology of those who stay or it drives away those whose principals are incorruptible. The good fight is too hard. In the end justice becomes whoever can afford the most skilled liar wins.

To whom are the perverters of the legal system culpable? No one. Our elected officials, who make laws and who are supposed to represent our views with laws that protect and maintain American ideals, are overwhelmingly drawn from the legal profession. They are far too worried over their campaign finances, their insider contacts, and their historical legacies to give a rip about my lost faith in their ability to effectively do their jobs. Why should they care about what I think? I am a minority in America. I am a lowly voter. Worse still, I am in the super-minority as a voter who knows the issues important to me and who does not rely upon celebrity endorsements or political party endorsements to tell me who to vote for. I am such a rare American that I feel that I may be the only one left. I study all sides of an issue so that I can make an informed decision about that issue. When I talk politics with people I feel that everyone has lost his mind. No one can tell me what he thinks anymore. All anyone can do is regurgitate the lie that the craftiest spin-doctor has created.

Every problem in America can be traced back to lawyers and the way the legal system has been perverted. Our current system favors the best liar over the intended system of discovering fact. We do not listen to opposing views in America anymore. We do not research issues. We certainly do not change our minds, even in the face of overwhelming evidence contrary to our opinions. To do these things is weak. What we believe today is whatever we are told to believe by the guy who signs the biggest check. I for one am sick of it.

It may seem that my focus has shifted from the broken legal system to the broken system of government but the focus has not shifted because the two separate problems are actually one in the same. Most people feel overwhelmed by the system and think that they cannot make a difference. No, I must be realistic. Most people do not care about the corruption in the government as long as they can watch paternity tests and secret transvestitism on trash talk shows. Most of the people who care enough to vote feel overwhelmed by the corruption in the system. The easy cash that permeates the backrooms quickly inundates those who feel they can enter the political arena and fix the broken system from the inside. Idealists are jaded in the process of creating politicians and power lawyers. There is no easy fix but there is a fix.

Drop your party loyalty. Politicians do not represent you. You, as a voter, are the mean to the end of a personal power grab. If you want to change the system stop voting for incumbents. Exposure to the system warps representatives' perspectives so keep that door revolving. Keep new idealistic blood pumping into the system. Do not ever elect representatives to consecutive terms. Until our representatives in government remember what it is like to be regular people, they will never truly represent us. Until we get law makers who will restore the idea of justice to our legal system my contempt for the current system would get me into real trouble under oath unless I could bring myself to lie convincingly like a true power grabber.

More Bad Words

When I was young, just like most kids, I was not allowed to say bad words. Unlike most kids my list of words that I could not say included words like poop and fart. When speaking of such bodily functions I used the words "acky" and "windy." Just because I did not say bad words that did not mean that I did not know them, yet I did not know all that I thought I knew.

On television and in movies people often referred to the "f" word. From the way that people spoke of the "f" word I was led to believe that it was the worst word that anyone could possibly say. Try though I may I could not, for the life of me, figure out what could possibly be so bad about fart. I knew it was a word that I was not allowed to say but I also knew that it was a word that other kids my age were allowed to say. I knew that there were other bad words that I had heard that seemed to me to be much worse than the "f" word because first, I had only ever heard grown-ups say these words and second, when I heard a grown-up saying those words they were usually mad. The "f" word by contrast was usually spoken with a smile if not a full laugh and usually spoken with mock anger that even I could differentiate from real anger at that tender age.

By the time I made it to Kindergarten, my Dad felt the need to sit me down and have a little talk with me. Although through the fog of years what I write that he said is probably not verbatim, it is pretty close. Dad said, "Now I know when you are off with your friends it's 'cool' to say cuss words." I was about to mount a furious protest when he pushed on saying, "That's all fine and good but I don't want to here any of that kind of language around here." That was the day I started saying bad words. It was also the day I started living my double life. There was the way John spoke when he was home and there was the way John spoke when he was with his friends.

Having a longer history than most with licentious word usage I have honed a vocabulary that has literally had a truck driver and later a drunken construction worker tell me, "Maybe you ought to watch your language son." This is not a source of pride, mind you, with difficulty and only moderate success I have attempted to remove the salt from my language.

I did have an interesting occasion when my Mom came into my bedroom one day and in a concerned voice said, "John, Aimee tells me you cuss when you are away from home." Aimee is my sister and my junior by two years. I respond to my Mom, "Yeah, I do." The concern is replaced with perplexity when Mom says, "But why?" I respond with the only thing I can think of, "Dad said I could." By the way, this conversation with my Mom took place when I was eighteen.

I have by now, of course, found out what the true "f" word is. I stand by my previous thought that I still do not think it is the worst word you can say. As a matter of fact, I believe firmly in the idea that there are no such things as bad words only bad intentions. I do, however, realize that most people do believe in the existence of bad words so I continue to try to temper my lascivious tongue. Perhaps I should bring my father along with me everywhere I go because to this day I am very uncomfortable using profanity in front of him. Now that I have my own children I would love for my words to them to carry the same weight that my Dad's words always carried with me. I know that they do not and I know that they will not but one can always hope.

Foniks

I hav hurd it sed that we shuld skrap r entir sistem of spelin wurdz and udopt a set of universal rools that wil mak redin and ritin English e-z-er. After al, we baro wurds and frazes frum so mane uther langwajez that kepin al uf thu disparut rools and aplikashuns strat iz nerle a frutles indevr for even thu most ardent bibleofil. Frum thu plural form uv mouse, ox, goose, elk, cactus, and hypothesis too thu miread uv silent leters that can be fownd in wurdz such az knight, gnu, pterosaur, comb, scythe, and phlegm we must konkur spelin terurz that riterz uv uther langwajez ned not kunsidr. Wut we hav her iz, falyur to elusidat. Just imajin thu fredum for intelectual pursoots that wuld opin too r children if we did not wast thu majorite uv ther prim edyukabl yers kramin thim ful uv nonsensikal rools for spelin.

Befor al uv thu retird English techrs brak owt thos flamibl efijes I wuld lik too point owt wun fakt in mi defens. Langwaj iz not rel. Wut I men too sa iz that kurekt langwaj iz not rel. Langwaj bi it's vere natyur iz flooid, abl too chanj it's aplikashun az ned arizez. English iz a derivutiv langwaj just az thu primare langwaj frum wich

English wuz derivd morfd intoo a vareashun uv an evn erleer langwaj. This iz not evn mi point, howevr. Thu rools uv r langwaj r kreatd and reinforsd bi usaj. *Fo pa* and taboo wurd yoosaj slidz intoo manstrem and eventyul skolrly akseptans if we r persistent and dilijent in r yoos uv thu langwaj in waz that fel rit rathr than thu waz we r told too yooz it. Ther wuz a tim wen it wuz unhurd uv too end a sentens with a preposishun. Toda, I culd not imajin frasing this kweschun difrentle, "So, war r u frum?" I can refras this kweschun too kunform too thu roolz uv Standrd English but we sa it rong so much that thu "korekt" wa iz no longr thu rit wa.

If u r havin trubl redin this, u can thank a techr for helpin u throo thu malstrum uv pedantre that iz thu English langwaj. Tak hart frum thu fakt that wil r wurld iz chanjin al arownd us in, sumtimz, inkonsevabl waz, r langwaj wil not be konverting too ane ezile kompatibl sistem uv foniks anetim in thu ner fyoochur. Besidz thu fakt that mane uv r letrs, most importantle thu vowls, mak mor than 1 sownd so we wuld hav too kreat noo letrs too akomodat; or we wuld hav too yooz thu letrs with thu markings abuv them in thu pronunsiashun sekshun uv thu dikshunare. E-thur wa this "fiks" wuld introdus mor problems in thu langwaj.

Uv cors, u wil hav too wure abowt this chanj cuming intoo f-ect. Wil Amerika iz thu kuting ej in triing noo thingz, we also hav a grat desir too mantan nostaljik if obsolet institushuns. If u r mi aj and espeshale if u r a litl oldr u remembr thu debakl wen we wer having thu metrik sistem forsed upon us. In ordr too wen us frum r arkaic sistem uv meshur, "thu man" desided too ad interstat distanses in kilometrs along with thu distans in milz. Ther wuz such baklash abowt thu mas confushun uv thu xtra numbrs on thu sins that thu metrik drem wuz lost, mabe 4 good. Aparentle, hiwa speds r not kondusiv too performing evn rudimentare mathematikal kalkulashuns.

Fer not kurmujuns, we wil not doo awa with r often inkomprehensibl sistem uv riting. We wil kontinyoo too atempt too fil children'z hedz with thu mas uv kunflikting roolz and nemonik devises that wil kep them frum evr caching thu rest uv thu wurld in math and siense.

Phonics

I have heard it said that we should scrap our entire system of spelling words and adopt a set of universal rules that will make reading and writing English easier. After all, we borrow words and phrases from so many other languages that keeping all of the disparate rules and applications straight is nearly a fruitless endeavor for even the most ardent bibliophile.

From the plural form of mouse, ox, goose, elk, cactus, and hypothesis to the myriad of silent letters that can be found in words such as knight, gnu, pterosaur, comb, scythe, and phlegm we must conquer spelling terrors that writers of other languages need not consider. What we have here is, failure to elucidate. Just imagine the freedom for intellectual pursuits that would open to our children if we did not waste the majority of their prime educable years cramming them full of nonsensical rules for spelling.

Before all of the retired English teachers break out those flaming effigies I would like to point out one fact in my defense. Language is not real. What I mean to say is that correct language is not real. Language by it's very nature is fluid, able to change it's application as need arises. English is a derivative language just as the primary language from which English was derived morphed into a variation of an even earlier language. This is not even my point, however. The rules of our language are created and reinforced by usage. *Fax pas* and taboo word usage slides into mainstream and eventual scholarly acceptance if we are persistent and diligent in our use of the language in ways that feel right rather than the ways we are told to use it. There was a time when it was unheard of to end a sentence with a preposition. Today I could not image phrasing this question differently, "So, where are you from?" I can rephrase this question to conform to the rules of Standard English but we say it wrong so much that the "correct" way is no longer the right way.

If you are having trouble reading this, you can thank a teacher for helping you through the maelstrom of pedantry that is the English language. Take heart from the fact that while our world is changing all around us in, sometimes, inconceivable ways, our language will not be converting to any easily compatible system of phonics anytime in the near future. Many of our letters, most importantly the vowels, make more that one sound so we would have to create new letters to accommodate; or we would have to use the letters with the markings above them in the pronunciation section of the dictionary. Either way this "fix" would introduce more problems into the language.

Of course, you will not have to worry about this change coming into effect. While America is the cutting edge in trying new things, we also have a great desire to maintain nostalgic if obsolete institutions. If you are my age and especially if you are a little older you remember the debacle when we were having the metric system forced upon us. In order to wean us from our archaic system of measure, "the man" decided to add interstate distances in kilometers along with the distance in miles. There was such backlash about the mass confusion of the extra numbers on the signs that the metric dream was lost, maybe for good. Apparently, highway speeds are not conducive to performing even rudimentary mathematical calculations.

Fear not curmudgeons, we will not do away with our often incomprehensible system of writing. We will continue to attempt to fill children's heads with the mass of conflicting rules and mnemonic devises that will keep them from ever catching the rest of the world in math and science.

Irregardless

If in fact irregardless was a word, it would mean not regardless, which does not make any sense, which is why it is not a word. You do not add a prefix to cancel a suffix from a word. The prefix "-Ir" means not and the suffix "-Less" means without. Place both on the base word regard and the resulting word means regard. This type of meaning cancellation can be employed to create an entire language of words that we do not need because we already have the original base word.

Unworthless could mean that something has value. We could describe things that have a definite beginning or end by calling them infiniteless. Klutzes can be called ungraceful. I could be referred to as not unbeautifulless. We could create such an incomprehensible array of meaning canceling prefix and suffix combinations that no one could discern our intended meaning. This could be incredibly useful to politicians, lawyers, and many practitioners of other undespicableless careers.

The purpose of language is to accurately and understandably transmit information. In order for communication to have transpired someone must send an intended message and someone else must have understood the meaning of that message. For this reason, I contend that slang is a perfectly acceptable form of communication provided that the sender and the receiver both understand the intended meaning of the nonstandard communication.

I believe that there is no such thing as a generation gap in America only a communication gap. Old people are nostalgia junkies dreaming of a bygone day when they were important and people listened to what they had to say. Young people are stimulus junkies dreaming of the far off day when they will be important and they can do all of the things they want to do and people will listen to what they have to say. Middle-aged people are leisure time junkies dreaming of a career where their personal interests are important but if they make a mistake it is not the end of the world and people stop expecting them to have all of the answers and know just what to say. Most of life is pining over what you used to have, wanting what you do not yet have, and wanting to give up the responsibilities that you currently have.

Old, young, and in between people are the same. However, we do not recognize our similarities because of the fluidity of language. We all have the same hopes and fears but we lack the commonality of expression to communicate from generation to generation. So, in the spirit of unity I offer the following bit of useful translations.

He's somethin' like a beast.
He's bitchin'.
He is a jim dandy.

Bling bling Tommy.
Thomas is a metrosexual.
Look at the fop.

Gimme dem drawers.
Free love, baby.
I just enlisted. I may not come back alive.

Pimp is a good thing.
Bad is a good thing.
Good is a good thing.

We are all the same we only speak a bit differently. We also believe that our own way of speaking is perfectly acceptable while other's slang usage is not.

I really do not have as much of a problem with people using irregardless as I do with the fact that they use it incorrectly. Invariably, when someone says irregardless he means regardless, which is the exact opposite of what he said. I find that people who say irregardless are the same people who say suposably, exspecially, and mischeavious. Although it is probably too late, I do not want to seem like a snooty bibliophile. I truly find the variations of language usage fascinating. While reading a dictionary—not the whole thing I'm not some kind of dictionary reading wierdo—I was amused by the passage that read they had seventy "experts" who weighed in on the proper spelling, pronunciation, and meaning of many of the words in the dictionary. Apparently there is some kind of hot academic disagreement, among people who do not have a handle on what real life is about, as to whether unalienable or inalienable is the proper usage. I can imagine a gray bearded man with an unlit pipe in his mouth and patches on the elbows of his slightly rumpled tweed jacket smacking a bespectacled woman wearing tan orthopedic shoes in the back of the head with a folding chair screaming, "Unalienable you mindless nitwit," every time I read 67% of our panel agree that unalienable is the preferred usage.

Even "experts" do not know what is right. Please do not think that I believe what I say is right and everyone else is wrong. I am reminded of the time I came across a word in a book I had never seen before. As near as I could tell by the context clues voila had exactly the same meaning as wah-la. I was mortified when I relayed my new discovery to my English teacher and it dawned on me at the exact same time he was telling me that wah-la is the way idiots like myself say voila. I then hit him in the head with a folding chair.

Maxims Explained

Number 3 was my attempt to sound profound and I apologize for it whole-heartedly. It came to me one day when I was walking in an unfamiliar city. Rather than watching where I was going I was looking at the architecture of the old buildings containing the local storefronts. It always amazes me how the absolutely beautifully made buildings of the past become the low rent establishments of today. Anyway, while looking near the top of a building I tripped over a section of sidewalk that had been tented by the roots of an old tree. At first I admonished myself for not watching where I was going and then I decided that the view had been worth the risk. I then puzzled out maxim number 3.

Number 4 is all of the dating advice that my Dad ever gave me. He said it in reference to a guy we knew who had beat up another guy for "fooling around" with his girlfriend. I believe Dad was saying that the woman is the one who has made a commitment to you and the blame for the infidelity lies with her. This is not to say you should beat up a wandering girlfriend but that beating up anyone does not fix the problem.

Numbers 5, 8, and 9 are some very early attempts, high school and even earlier, at some universal truths. They are not incredibly imaginative but I still believe in their truth so I have added them here. Creativity is developed over time and it is often helpful to start with someone else's words and then add your own. I like these additions because they show the progression of my abilities from stinking horrible to moderately horrible.

Number 20 was the comment written at the top of an essay returned to me by my Introduction to Shakespeare teacher in my junior year of college. I had the incredibly witty quip, "I wasn't exactly striving for verbosity and pomposity," but the scathing criticism has stuck in my mind for over a decade. I believe that I have overcome these faults even though my sister would disagree. Upon proofreading an early draft of the book for me, Aimee noted, "I am a teacher and I don't know some of the words you use. If I am running to the dictionary I am not reading your words." I have looked over this book carefully and the words I use were chosen for their precise shade of meaning and not because I want to exclude anyone from understanding. I refuse to assist in the dumbing down of American reading so the words remain.

It is my hope that the rest of the maxims are self evident in their meaning. If not, ask me some time. However, I would prefer talking about your thoughts on issues and specifically why you think what you think. People's reasoning is endlessly fascinating to me.

Thank You

Thank you very much for reading my book. My only hope is that you are glad that you read it. I mentioned early on that I do not have it all figured out and if you have read all of the pages between that page and this page then mentioning it to you again is sadly unnecessary. I hope you smiled while reading this book and I really hope you laughed out loud a time or two, and if at any moment a tear approached your eye or a frog threatened you throat, I hope it was not in painful memory of the money with which you parted in order to obtain this book.

I did not intend to change your mind with this book and I certainly did not intend to offend you. As a matter of fact, the only thing a person can do to get in my crawl is to take offense. You see, by taking offense to something someone else has written or said, you are proclaiming your opinion to be true and correct and all other opinions invalid. Part of the definition of opinion is that it cannot be proven correct or incorrect. I would truly like to unite people and if that union is only a unified disdain for me, and my presumption, I guess I still win.

I would like to give a special thank you to my wife, Shanah. For my birthday, four years ago, Shanah bought me a very nice ink pen, replacement ink cartridges, a three ring binder, and two packs of filler paper. Thank you for the faith in my writing and the implied permission to write those things rattling around in my head no matter how bizarre. I love you Shanah Lynn and I thank you. I do not believe I would have ever gotten around to writing this down without that perfect gesture inside the perfect gift. I learned how to write with the pen you gave me in the notebook you gave me nurtured in the love you gave me.

Thanks again to everyone and if this is a library book, I hope it was read in the living room or the bedroom. Have a little respect for the next person and do not take a library book into the bathroom.

AF
Callahan   Callahan, John.
                    Zen and the art
                    of whittling
                Athens Public
                Library (Ohio)
9-6-07

DATE DUE

SEP 2 6 2007		
OCT 0 4 2007 OCT 2 5 2007		
MAR 2 4 2011		
MAY 2 2 2013		
GAYLORD		PRINTED IN U.S.A.